THE SEASON OF DRAGONS

TANSY RAYNER ROBERTS

 Created with Vellum

For Caroline Bingley
who was robbed

CONTENTS

CHAPTER I
FIVE THOUSAND A YEAR.

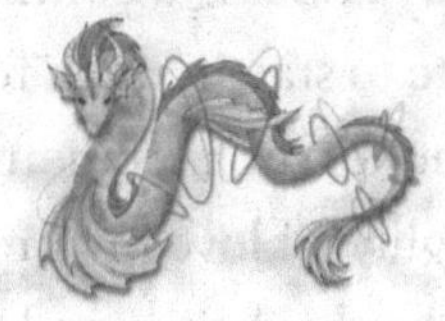

By far the worst thing that could happen to a gentleman of good family is to come into his fortune at the age of two-and-twenty. Why, a man of such recent vintage has barely begun forming his character, and now he shall never have to.

"When you say things like that, Dimity," clucked my sister Dido as I sulked on the window seat of her parlour, "It really does make you sound like a dragon."

I had not realised I was speaking my thoughts aloud, but having done so I was willing to stand by the sentiment. I hardly ever say things that I do not mean.

"I would be honoured to be a dragon," I said with fire in my heart. "Oh, I wish I were!"

"You'd have to give up bonnets," said Dido with a twinkle, busily knitting some garment or other for an impending baby (not her own, thank the Mother). "None would fit."

"Worth it," I vowed under my breath. "I'd sacrifice

1

half my bonnets right now if it meant Chambrey would change his mind about this horrid plan."

Dido raised her eyebrows and purled her stitch at the same time, which is quite the trick. "I suppose we *could* let him run off to play at being a country gent without us, if you're so desperate to stay in town for the Season..."

I stared wildly at her for a moment, and then we both burst into fits of laughter. I love my brother dearly, but it's bad enough that he has his hands on his funds so early in life — and that every fortune-hunter in the Nine Hundred knows he now has an income of five thousand a year.

The last thing Dido and I would ever do is let that sweet, innocent rabbit out of our sights. Not until he was safely settled with a suitable wife.

Thank goodness for Rackham. My sister and I were not the only valiant souls standing between Chambrey and the decade or so of terrible decisions he would surely have ahead of him without our diligence.

It's not that our brother was unintelligent, you understand, though please never tell him I said so. It was his tendency to believe the utter best in every person he has ever met that left him constantly teetering on the brink of the most dreadful peril.

For the sake of Chambrey and our family's future happiness, I had already resolved to sacrifice this Season. I would, however, begrudge and decry his wretched scheme every step of the way.

The Season in Abberline is quite the best time and place in the entire world. This is where the dragons gather when they awake from hibernation. Our city was founded on basalt and other types of volcanic rock that make it especially appealing to dragons — though I'm sure all the splendid parks, museums, ballrooms and theatres are also something of a drawcard!

For a few blissful months every year (the sweet spot between the final chill of winter and the first tiresome heat of summer), all our patrons and doyennes and inspirational elders condescend to emerge from hibernation in their shiniest scale and claw to make the world marvellous with their presence.

Granite statues crack their jewelled eyes open. Colour floods back into their sun-warmed flesh. All around the country, our cave-dwelling aunts and godfathers and patronesses stretch their wings, yawn and hurl themselves into flight.

Why would you wish to be anywhere else?

Summer is for hunting and autumn is for hoarding. Winter is for the long rest: for dreaming of next year's invitation lists and dinner menus and theatrical commissions. But spring...

Spring is the season of dragons. And thanks to my thoughtless brother, I was going to miss it!

OUR PARENTS DIED when Chambrey and I were only fifteen. Luckily, our older sister Dido had made a decent match with Mr Harefield the previous year, and was already established in her own household in Gosling Square. If not for that, Chambrey and I might have found ourselves quite adrift, as our family's patroness had been asleep for seven years at that point, and dear Papa never did purchase a family estate to hand down to my brother, though he could well afford it.

There was an estate somewhere in the North, and a handful of other properties associated with our esteemed family patron, the Countess. But she had lost them, long before forming a connexion with our family.

My grandfather Iverwold was a self-made man, who left home to seek his fortune and happened upon a wounded, dying wyvern whose family and hoard had been taken from her by hunters. He saved her life, she accepted his fealty, and thus they were bound together forever. Together, they built a fortune anew, hoarding enough to restore her public standing and earn him a society marriage.

My father inherited a fortune and the Countess, whose wise counsel enabled him to marry well and build his fortune even higher, while she built a new hoard more magnificent than the one she had lost — this one lodged securely in a vault below the Bank of Abberline because she had been burned once before.

A gentleman should have an estate, especially a gentleman with a family, and the benevolent patronage of a dragon. Papa knew this. But like his father before him, he hesitated to tie up funds in property — at least, until he found the perfect home, which proved to be elusive.

Our childhood was spent in a series of progressively grander rented townhouses in the best streets of Abberline, punctuated by visits to country homes owned by family friends — at the proper time of year for such visits, which is to say anything but spring!

The finest of all country houses is Malachite, belonging to Chambrey's dear friend Mr Fordyce Rackham, himself the son of Papa's dear friend (also named Mr Fordyce Rackham). While our Rackham is five years older, his kind condescension to Chambrey in our youth has turned into a genuine friendship in adulthood. He was not able to join our family as *some of us* might have wished (I once cherished hopes that Rackham and Dido would find a match together, but neither fell prey to my schemes), he is honorary family, and I am really rather fond of him.

I also delight in Rackham's sister Tatiana, whom I have known since she was a toddler in ruffled drawers. I have many happy memories of us all roaming around the lake in the grounds of Malachite together as the most amiable horde of youngsters.

I once heard Chambrey joke with Rackham that Papa was never going to purchase an estate of his own until he found one quite as magnificent as Malachite, and Rackham replied in that rather dry manner of his "Well, that explains why he has been making handsome offers of purchase to me since I was twelve years old."

Rackham and Tatiana were orphaned even earlier than us, which is a good reason for the Rackhams and Iverwolds to stick together in a fierce circle of mutual protection. It has proven a most beneficial connexion over the years: when Chambrey is being simply impossible, Mr Rackham can usually be relied upon to talk sense into him.

Except, as it happens, in the matter of the Country Gentleman Scheme, which none of us were able to prevent.

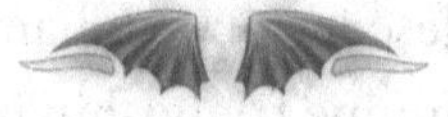

Two days into the Season, and Abberline came alive. Several of my old school chums (those whose families never popped their nose into the metropolis until there was a chance of someone's parasol being set alight) had already returned to their townhouses and begun the usual delightful mash of paying calls, exchanging gossip and plotting to see as many dragons as possible.

Kitty Hendricks was simply dying to take a turn about Hydde Park with me, so we might pay our respects to the Countess. We had planned it for Saturday, to allow the Serpentyne to properly fill up with water drakes. From there we would take tea and cake at the British Museum, to see if the legendary Hydra was showing her first blush.

The Ladies of the Coterie would not accept petitions for new members until later in the month, and no rumours had yet been dropped as to which of the grandest and oldest of the city's dragons would host the first ball of the Season.

This was only the second year that my sister would have allowed me to attend the Pleasure Gardens at night, with its displays of fireworks, air-dancing and the Flame Regiment!

So many parties were to be delicately planned, discussed and put into action over the next few weeks.

With Chambrey's eligibility as a matrimonial prospect finally coming into bloom, Dido and I would have received more invitations this year than we knew what to do with! (He was too young, of course, to be properly settled, but we could begin refining our list of prospects, and certainly enjoy the perquisites of having such a marriageable young man on our hands).

I was going to miss it all. My foolish twin had got it into his head that being a Gentleman of Significance with full access to his money meant *this* was the occasion to hire himself a country house in the middle of nowhere and ruin my life.

I should not blame Rackham. Our dear friend had done his best. I still recall the rather strained notes in his voice when Chambrey first unveiled his scheme.

"[Something]—shire," said Rackham politely, while I tried not to swoon in distress. (He might as well have said Nothing-shire.) "My dear fellow, what on earth is in [Something]-shire?"

"Us!" declared Chambrey with a merry smile. "I've taken a house, and we shall all go down together."

"Even Mr Harefield?" inquired Dido in a tone of mild horror.

"If he should wish it, sister, he is more than welcome! It shall be such fun."

We all looked at Dido's husband, who addressed himself to the dinner plate before him and ignored us all, which we took to mean that he would join us in [Something]-shire without complaint, though he should all rather we stayed at home.

Rackham considered his own chop and peas in deep thought before making a quiet reply. "Shall it, indeed?"

"Ah, you can't fool me!" said Chambrey, still grinning as if he had presented us all with a marvellous treat. "You detest town, dear fellow, and far prefer the country."

"I do not deny it," said Rackham like the gracious gentleman he was. "Though there are many amusements in town at this time of year, do you not think?"

That was for my benefit, and I loved him dearly for making the effort — we all knew that Rackham desired no city amusements himself beyond a quiet perambulation in an art gallery or two, and the occasional dinner at his club. The Season held little allure for him, but he showed no disrespect to those who consumed its delights with passionate zeal. He always asked me how I had spent my day, with all the proper pretence of interest in what I had to report.

"...but if it is country air that calls you, old friend," Rackham continued like a dashing hero from one of those novels about knights and castles, "Could you and I not retire to Malachite for a few weeks, and leave the ladies to their engagements?"

"No, no!" burst out Chambrey. "This will not do. For decades you, and your father before you, have generously hosted our family in comfort and consideration. Now that I finally have the means to return the favour, would you deny me that opportunity?"

I saw a rare moment of weakness cross Rackham's craggy visage; he was weakening. "The gift is in your company, which I enjoy best in the world," he said in a rather small voice for a gentleman who has been striding with confidence through the world since he was in short trousers. "Not in my humble hospitality."

"Then," said Chambrey, in an unexpectedly winning move for a gentleman who has never stayed awake through a game of chess in his life. "Allow me to be self-ish, dear fellow, and enjoy that gift for myself."

At which point, the traitor Rackham conceded his territory in the name of eternal friendship, and I stabbed my potatoes viciously with a fork.

It was up to me, the youngest of the party, to make a final plea for sense. I held my tongue until pudding was served. "Brother," I murmured over a dish of cherry clafoutis and seared custard. "*Must* your quarter-life crisis occur at this precise moment? I'll have to cancel so many engagements and merry plots with my friends, and we'll miss the Vigil, and..."

"No," said Chambrey in a sharper tone than I deserved. "We will not miss the Vigil, Dimity, because we were never going to attend. The Vigil has nothing to offer our family but false hope. You must forget about the Countess and look forward. I'm sure you'll love the country. The people will be so charming."

My brother then took a deep breath, pasted a sunny smile on his face, and was perfectly amiable to us all through pudding, cheese and coffee, until he and Rackham could finally escape to billiards and ignore us ladies entirely.

The people will be so charming. Oh, Mother. Was he expecting us to make friends out there, in the land of swamps and sweetshops?

Dido and I could remain behind. There was no law that said we had to traipse obediently into the back of beyond because our brother was 'head of the family' or any such rot.

However, the upsetting truth was that Rackham had proved himself malleable to my brother's blandishments, and thus he could no longer be relied upon to guard Chambrey's virtue. One could not trust a single man in possession of a good fortune to be let out *unsupervised* in the country.

Chambrey Iverwold needed protection from the more grasping sort of fortune-hunter who might easily persuade him that he, at the tender age of two-and-twenty, was a bank vault in want of a wife.

He might not have a dragon to protect him, but he had two fierce sisters, and that was nearly as good.

CHAPTER 2
ELDERFLOWER HALL IS LET AT LAST

The loss of the Season weighed on me, I will admit, as our party set off in Chambrey's chaise-and-four. I sulked enough that Chambrey suggested I should take Mr Harefield's spot next to the driver, as if Mr Harefield would sacrifice an opportunity to avoid conversation with his wife and her relatives.

Dido set her own disappointment aside, proffering a dubious interest in the house where we were to stay.

Chambrey proved entirely unsatisfactory in describing Elderflower Hall and its surrounds, except for the supporting details that the hired estate was so many miles from Abberline, and that the nearby town of Merrywist was both 'charming' and 'quaint.'

"Of course it looks attractive," I muttered into the window of the chaise. "That's how they trap you. Ask any bee how it feels about the foxglove."

Dido rolled her eyes at me from behind her decorative fan; Rackham gave an amused snort.

MERRYWIST *WAS* both quaint and charming. As pretty as a chocolate box, and small in every respect: it could only be called a town rather than a village because it had *two* shopping streets, and it was clear that the residents were ill-accustomed to visitors from the city. The lavish jewel-toned paintwork of Chambrey's carriage, quite modest by the standards of girls I had been to school with, caught every eye as we passed through. I could practically hear the chain of gossip as it passed from haberdasher to greengrocer and beyond.

An alarming thought crossed my mind. "You have not yet called upon anyone, have you?"

Now it was my brother's turn to roll his eyes. "A few of the local gentlemen called on me in a friendly manner, to welcome Elderflower Hall's new tenant."

"And you called on them in return," I realised with a sinking feeling. "Already?" Without us to keep an eye on him, and prevent the wrong sort of friendship developing, was what I meant.

"Within a few days. It's how things are done, Dim."

"I know how things are done," I snapped.

Dido took over with those smooth hostess skills she had been honing her whole life. "Do any of these local gentlemen have daughters, my dear?"

Chambrey leaned back against the soft leather lining of the chaise. "What's wrong with daughters?"

"Don't be obtuse, Chambrey. You must be careful."

"I can assure you, Dido, I'm capable of sitting in a fellow's library for ten minutes without accidentally affiancing myself to his daughter."

"They move fast, in rural communities," Rackham said evenly. "Have you received any dinner invitations, Iverwold?"

"Sir Willem Ellis invited us all to dinner next week," muttered Chambrey, looking pleased with himself. "Capital fellow, he's connected to the Topaz flamedrakes, you know. And I had to turn down an invitation to dine with the Bellamy family a few days ago, because I was coming to Abberline to collect you all. But there's an assembly ball tomorrow, and we can all become acquainted with the locals."

"A country dance?" I inquired in a tone usually reserved for squashed flies on the window sill.

Dido nudged me with her foot, disapproving of my lack of subtlety. We couldn't all be diplomats!

"I've been assured that springtime in Merrywist is packed with entertainments and we won't miss Abberline at all," said Chambrey with a smile that I did not appreciate in the least.

Rackham snorted again, eyeing the empty fields we were passing on the way to our brother's new home.

"And how many unmarried daughters has the gentleman who said such a thing?" prodded Dido.

"Five," my brother admitted. He was enough of a good sport to join in, when all three of us laughed at him.

Elderflower Hall was pleasant enough, as houses go. Cold from years of being rented hither and thither, and even more years of *not* being rented out. There was little evidence yet of whatever family had originally lived here: no family portraits, or crests burned into the woodwork.

I could not even tell if a dragon had ever been in residence: the cellars were too newly restored to show antique scorch marks, or the usual wear and tear that a treasure hoard might leave upon grey flagstones after a century or two. I had my suspicions about the greenhouse, which had been constructed out of steel and glass without a splinter of wood, and was therefore flameproof. It certainly had the space to house a dragon, but there was no sign as to whether one had lived there recently, or even within the last fifty years.

The library was extensive, and yet there were no volumes referring to the house itself, or its history.

The park surrounding the hall was enormous, practically six parks altogether. Chambrey lost no opportunity in dragging Rackham and Harefield out to ride and stomp about in mud and gambol recklessly. Clearly, my brother had been holding himself back all these years, desperate to inhabit the life of a country gent — Rackham was pleased to indulge him, and Harefield approved of any activity that meant no one expected him to make conversation.

(The gentlemen were out of the house and in the saddle most days by the time I rose for breakfast at the civilised hour of nine. They were often still out when Dido and I met for a bite of nuncheon in the early afternoon. The very thought of what they were up to exhausted me.)

"Doesn't it bother you?" I asked Dido. "We don't know whether this house originally belonged to hoarders or hunters."

Dido considered her own thoughts over toast points and honey. "I can't see how it matters," she said. "It's an Iverwold house for as long as we live in it."

IVERWOLDS HAVE ALWAYS BEEN HOARDERS. It's in our blood; in our history. We care for our dragons, and we care for their jewels. Even with a grandfather in trade, even with a patroness in hibernation and no waking dragon to advise us, we are hoarders.

My grandfather came from a small town where dragons were considered sacred; long before we had a dragon of our own, we knew that protecting them was the most important thing a human could do.

You can be a hoarder, or a hunter. There is no middle ground.

If our family vault was emptied tomorrow, and nothing remained of the Countess's hoard but a single pearl, we would guard that pearl with our lives, and we would build our fortune back all over again without harming a single scale of a dragon's flesh. It is the only honourable way to live. (Even if two-fifths of the Nine Hundred do not agree.)

And so, when I learned that Mr Bellamy of the five daughters, who had called on Chambrey within days of his taking Elderflower Hall, and in whose library Chambrey had politely sat for ten minutes only a few days later... when I learned that he was a retired dragon hunter with fifteen kills on his record...

Well, I vowed then and there that Chambrey would only marry one of those five daughters over my dead body.

And that was before I met the horrid little fortune-hunters.

CHAPTER 3
ALL THESE COUNTRY DANCES BLUR TOGETHER

Assemblies, I am told, when one lives in and around a tiny thatched-roof town such as Merrywist, are a series of rustic gatherings in which the same five-and-twenty families gather to practice their galliards, and eat lukewarm savouries, while attempting with little tact or decorum to marry their children to each other.

This is not what I consider an assembly, but I suppose not every young gentlewoman gets to come out at a King Street ball sponsored by the Coterie. I'm well aware how lucky I have been, before my foolish brother snatched this Season away from me.

DURING THE FIRST fort-night we stayed at Elderflower Hall, we were invited to three assemblies, each as dire as the last. Were it not for the new hats that Dido's maid had trimmed for me with amberscale lace and cerise ribbons, I would have quite lost the will to live.

At home, Abberline would be bursting into life and fire as the dragons awoke, sending gold-edged invitations to blanket the city like the best kind of smog. I had already received two letters from Kitty Hendricks and three from Emma Watling, describing many of the marvels and gossip I had missed so far.

Here in Merrywist, our only consolation was a supper room full of moulded jellies and a town hall full of moulded gentlefolk, each of them placing bets on which of their beribboned local swindlers would get her grubby hands on my brother's fortune.

(I remain convinced, though Dido tells me I am being unkind, that two of the three assemblies, if not the whole set, came into existence purely because the locals were so excited at the appearance of a marriageable gentleman in the neighbourhood.)

At the first assembly, Chambrey danced every dance — a pair each with me and Dido, for the sake of respectability, then a pair with a daughter or two from each of the higher ranked families of the locality. Dido, who had quietly procured all manner of advanced intelligence by way of our new housekeeper, gardener and butcher's boy, ensured that he chose appropriately.

This was all well and good when it came to Miss Ellis, the daughter of the local squire, who was plain and intelligent-looking and thus no danger. Or even her younger sister Sophiar, who was slightly prettier but not of an age to be actively hunting a husband.

No, the danger came from an entirely different direction: that family with the five unmarried daughters. Mr Bellamy, Chambrey had assured us, was a capital fellow with a dry wit. What he had not revealed is that the family were from a long line of hunters.

I'm sure we looked quite the snobs, standing stiffly in our formal lace and linens while this raucous family tipped into the assembly hall behind us. But once I recognised the tiara pinned to the curls of the eldest daughter, I found it hard to breathe, let alone make the usual polite courtesies.

Rackham froze like a statue at the sight of it. I did not blame him in the least.

While it is true that many of today's fashions are inspired by our country's love of dragons — witness my amberscale lace, perfectly replicating the popular scooped pattern found on many a dragon's flank — we have moved beyond the grotesqueries of the past, such as the outdated tradition of wearing trophies from our family's history of murder and cruelty.

At least, those from *our* sort of family have moved on. Apparently the daughters of dragon hunters found it perfectly appropriate to wear the spoils of their sport to a country dance.

Miss Leda Bellamy, the eldest daughter, wore a tiara that had to be a century old — completely out of fashion — and glittered with diamond scales from a dead jewelback. Jewelback dragons were mostly extinct these days, because so many hunters had murdered them for these trinkets.

It was not inappropriate to keep such an object in one's family hoard, in respectful acknowledgement of the sad crimes of the past. But in Abberline, anyone who wore such an item in public would be cut direct — and would find every dance invitation for the next five years dry up like dust on the wind.

"People do things differently in the country," murmured Chambrey, patting my arm as if worried I was about to leap into action and tear the wretched tiara from the horrid Bellamy girl's head. "Not everyone can afford new jewels."

"Then they should not wear jewels," I hissed, my nails pressing into Dido's wrist.

"Iverwold," said Rackham in a hoarse voice. "What exactly do you know about that Bellamy fellow?"

"Why, that his eldest daughter is dashed pretty," said Chambrey, a sulky tone taking him over. "And I shall dance with her as many times as I am allowed!"

Now that we came to examine them, every Bellamy daughter had some kind of distressing trophy pinned at her bosom, her throat or her hair. One wore pearls threaded around a single opaltooth. Another wore a copper locket embedded with the kind of amethyst that can only be mined from the eye socket of a hibernating hydra.

The mother, who was loud and exuberant, ushering her daughters this way and that as if they were princesses of the realm, carried an antique purse of embroidered wyvern silk, an elegant term for a product made from flattened wing skin.

As for the father — retired gentleman he might be, but this was a formal occasion, and so he wore the sash that displayed his shameful career for all to see — fifteen dragons dead at his hand.

I have known hunter families before — several of them sent their daughters to my school — but there was usually a sense of restraint when they moved in polite society. Discretion about their bloodstained history.

The Bellamy family were entirely shameless about their origins. Clearly a popular group, they were warmly greeted by friends and acquaintances as they paraded around the hall. No one seemed to find their dress the least bit distasteful.

Thank goodness the gathering was deprived of spare gentlemen; none of the locals approached me to dance, protected as I was between my sister and her husband.

Chambrey tried to encourage Rackham to join him in frolicking through the five and twenty families of the Merrywist social whirl, but Rackham sensibly demurred.

BY THE SECOND ASSEMBLY, six days later — another week of Abberline revels missed, in order that Dido and I might take tea in a draughty manor while our gentlemen enjoyed long muddy walks and contemplated the benefits of owning more than one dog! — we were prepared for the worst.

I had been asking a great many questions, spending enough money (and time) at the milliner's, the circulating library and even the sweet shop to gather local gossip. That was how I learned that there were hardly any dragons living in this county. Society dragons, that was — oh, there were a few distant aunts or godfathers who occasionally flew through, but this was a rarity. The Ellises had a patron, but she was in long hibernation, and rarely made a public appearance when awake. As for the rest of them — what dragons had dwelled here once had long since crawled away into the mountains, or let themselves fall into permanent sleep, eternally stone.

No wonder the people of Merrywist threw country dances without any sense of originality or style. This was a town bereft, drifting along without the proper guidance of their betters.

(This also explained how the Bellamy family could wear their tacky battle souvenirs without social consequence.)

The second assembly was less of a shock to the system, now that I knew what to expect. Those Bellamy girls must have a limited selection of gory ornaments with which to pair their home-trimmed gowns, and I had quite braced myself to see the dreadful items on display all over again.

The ghastly mother was no better on this occasion; no amount of preparation was sufficient for greetings to be hollered at us from afar (Mrs Bellamy never moved once she had found a comfortable seat at a public event, expecting her family to run around fetching her drinks and sweetmeats for all the world as if she was her family's patron dragon).

Whomever had raised Mrs Bellamy (and she did seem to have some formal courtesies about her!) had never taught her to be discreet about her opinions. She visibly twitched with tactless annoyance when Mr Rackham did not fall over himself to compliment her or her daughters. She almost strained herself in switching from grumpy to sunshine when Chambrey swept by with the eldest Miss Bellamy in his arms.

I thawed enough to make polite conversation with some of the locals this time around. Miss Sophiar , younger daughter of the local squire Sir Willem Ellis, was a charming little thing, complimenting my lace in a stumbling manner. She later confessed over lemonade that the town had been rife with rumours ahead of our arrival, to the point that they expected my brother to bring a party of *twelve* ladies and *seven* gentlemen to the hall with him.

"Goodness," I said without much thought. "How extraordinary to imagine so many might travel away from civilisation at this time of year."

Sophiar coloured a little, and it occurred to me later that she might have thought it an insult.

I danced with Mr Rackham, each of us agreeing in furious undertones about how dreadful it was that the local gentry were tripping over themselves to hurl their daughters at my brother and his five thousand a year. He was greatly relieved that the same locals had dismissed Rackham himself as too disagreeable to be worth his far greater fortune.

"If only dragons had learned how a scowling countenance is the best way to turn fortune hunters from their caves," I teased him. "How many more might be still alive today?"

"It is a useful shield," Mr Rackham confessed with the ghost of a smile.

"Malachite is bordered by four villages," I said as the thought occurred to me. "Do they make you dance, and throw daughters at your head?" Rackham was always less grouchy at home, though he had never insisted we join him at a single local assembly.

"I cut the occasional ribbon for them," he admitted. "And judge the village fairs when called upon. But none of my local gentry have marriageable daughters, and so I am quite safe from dancing and supper parties except when visiting my aunt."

I shivered at the mention of his aunt. All dragons must be revered and respected above all things, but some are downright terrifying, and Lady Beautrice de Bramble was one of those.

After our pair of dances, Mr Rackham and I were free to stand and survey the room, sharing light and amusing observations of the rabble until Chambrey pounced upon us. "Rackham!" he exclaimed. "I must have you dance."

"You know what a punishment it is for me," Rackham

grumbled. "Meeting new people is bad enough, but to stand up with fresh acquaintances?"

I tweaked the sleeve of his jacket. "Such a chore it is to learn new names and their father's professions and think of three original things to say about the same lavender muslin gown made over in six different ways. How you must suffer under the weight of it."

"Please," said Rackham. "No true gentleman has less than six prepared statements about lavender muslin ready to go at any given time. Luckily for us all, no dance in the land is long enough to provide the opportunity to share *three* original thoughts."

"I don't understand the pair of you," said Chambrey, who had never developed the ability to read sarcasm. "I love to chat during a dance. One can find out so many things about another person when one is genuinely interested."

"Yes," I said, my humour taking on a sour note. "I imagine you have gathered dozens of facts of interest about Miss Bellamy by now. Must you dance with her so many times? You'll give her mother ideas."

"If Rackham would dance with more local ladies, I would not feel so obliged to make up the difference," Chambrey scolded.

"Yes, I'm sure my participation would regulate yours," Rackham sighed. "But as you have monopolised the only pretty girl in the room..."

I stepped on his foot.

"...present company excepted..."

"Too slow, Mr Rackham," I said, and opened my fan

with a flutter. "I'll leave you to your assessment of the locals, but please, brother, try to dance with *someone* who hasn't matched her ballgown to a slice of dead dragon before the night is over."

I LATER HEARD that a different Bellamy daughter — Laura, the one with the eye socket amethyst — spent most of the evening mocking Mr Rackham for being too proud to dance with the local girls.

It was all I could do not to scratch her eyes out.

IT SHOULD HARDLY BE a surprise to this reader that I had no wish for my brother to chuse a bride in this oubliette, far from proper society. If I were to be held with a musket to my head and forced to chuse, however, my preference would be Miss Allicot Ellis, Sophiar's elder sister — and as it happened, their father, Sir Willem, hosted the fortnight's third assembly (more of a tea party, really, with a few set dances in the drawing room, but I was kind enough not to call attention to that fact in front of anyone — it was clear by now that our new neighbours were to be pitied, not scorned).

Miss Ellis might not be as pretty as Leda Bellamy and her sisters, but she was capable of making clever conversation, and actually took an interest in the world beyond Merrywist. She made quite a contrast to Miss Bellamy, who stood in a frozen manner when addressed, only showing the faintest glimmer of warmth when my brother spoke to her directly (and even then, hiding most of her face behind a lace fan).

More to the point, the Ellis family were hoarders, not hunters, which made me far more comfortable under their roof than I would have been in other local houses. Their patron, the gracious Great Aunt Agatha, sneered grandly down at us from an oil painting in the hallway, her wings spread wide and a beaded lace fichu adorning her sapphire chest scales.

"She only awakes from hibernation every three or four years now," Miss Ellis told me in a murmur, looking rather wistful. "I had hoped the promise of a party might lure her out of the greenhouse. Next year, perhaps."

It was an anxious time, when an ageing dragon was due to emerge from hibernation and chose to skip one more spring and summer. No one knew better than I how that felt, though I could never entirely shut away the hope as Chambrey did that this year might be different.

Our Countess might be awake right now, and none of her human family there to greet her!

Yes, Miss Ellis was promising. Sadly, she was twenty-seven years old and had so thoroughly resigned herself to spinsterhood that she barely even tried to catch Chambrey's eye. As soon as the Bellamys made their entrance to the Ellis assembly (late as usual, the younger two sisters still arguing as they strode in, as if this was some common or garden chophouse and not a respectable home), I winced to see my brother's face light up like a lamppost.

Miss Ellis saw it too and turned away with a smile even more wistful than the one she had worn when discussing her family's sleeping dragon.

"Do engagements move more quickly in the country?" I murmured to Dido in the supper room, as I watched Chambrey fill a plate of refreshments for Miss Bellamy, picking radishes out of a perfectly satisfactory salad in order to please her.

Miss Bellamy had left her grotesque tiara at home for once and was gazing at him like he had conquered an army.

"I'm sure there's no danger," said Dido from behind her fan, though I could see she was biting her lip. "You know Chambrey. He's enthusiastic about *everyone*."

I thought this to be far too optimistic, and I could see from the crease in Rackham's brow that he agreed with me.

The situation was rapidly tumbling towards *precarious*.

CHAPTER 4
FORTUNE-HUNTERS AND FINE EYES

from Kitty Hendricks:

My dearest Dimity

I scarcely know where to begin, as you have missed so many of this Season's great moments already! Myfanwy Highwater's Great Aunt Edith awoke Saturday last and strode down Bond Street with her scales gleaming and her talons wet with ink. Such a magnificent sight, with several members of the Highwater family scampering along behind, holding up parasols to prevent her from burning in the spring sunshine. She is quite a lovely lavender-violet colour, and I suppose they want to preserve it long enough for Myfanwy and her sisters to order matching dresses for the

from Emma Watling:

Dimity, you will be quite overcome when I inform you that Mrs Walpole is awake and has scratched invitations for three balls in King Street already! You must take some comfort my poor darling in the news that you were invited to every single one of them! One of our maids ran into one of Mrs Harefield's maids at the haberdasher's and said that invitations have been simply piling up in her front hall, all addressed to you! Oh, I wish you could

"That's it," I said, casting aside the letters I had received from Kitty and Emma that morning. "I'm ruined. This was *my* Season."

"Oh, my dear," said Dido, giving me a sympathetic look. "You have plenty of time to find your place in society, and the best of husbands."

"Not if I'm here, slowly turning into garden mulch in the country while the city comes to life," I moaned. "Some of these invitations might never come again!"

Mr Rackham gave me a gentle glower from over his

plate of kedgeree. "You have been fussing for weeks, Dimity, about Chambrey being too young to marry. How on earth can you, as his twin sister, be on the shelf?"

I gaped at him, quite horrified at what had come out of his mouth. "Mr Rackham. I did not say on the shelf, and even if I was on the shelf, actually saying it out loud is beyond the pale! You know that it's different for ladies."

He smirked at me. "I think you have a few seasons yet before you need to worry."

I shot him a grouchy look and then fluttered my letters open again, returning to Emma's.

There are rumours that Mr Leonidas has engaged himself secretly to one of the Thistlegrass sisters, and no one knows which one, but all of them have been invited to Lady Dorchester's pearl hunt in the Wyvern Gardens! I shall have a new bonnet and Kitty

"If Chambrey marries Miss Bellamy," I said in a small voice. "There are several families in Abberline from whom I would never receive an invitation ever again."

There were hunter families in the city; of course there were. But those who took part in the social whirl of the Nine Hundred knew how to be discreet about the sources of their wealth; they treated the dragons of Society with respect no matter what they might get up to in the mountains, or while tracking wild wyverns through distant lands. Meanwhile, Emma's Papa was an outspoken member of Parliament who championed rights for rural dragons; Kitty's older sister had been cut off when she eloped with a hunter.

If my brother wed a country girl who thought it appropriate to wear battle trophies with a ballgown, while her mother boasted in public about her family's legendary kills, many of my closest friends and connexions could turn to dust on the wind.

Rackham attacked his breakfast with a fork as if it had insulted his aunt. "He's not going to marry her," he said firmly. "It's not that serious."

THE FUNNY THING IS, if I were to pick a Bellamy sister who might attract Chambrey, I would have thought Laura — the sharp-edged & mocking second eldest — far more of a danger. Chambrey has always been drawn to those more intelligent and cutting than himself — hence the surprisingly close friendship that exists between himself and Mr Rackham.

(Outsiders are often surprised at the bond between the two men, considering the difference in years, lack of shared school experience, and their deeply contrasting personalities. Having watched their friendship unfold in real time, I can confirm it was rather like watching a tiny kitten charm a haughty stallion.)

Miss Leda, if she shared her sister's searing wit, was keeping it well under wraps.

Today's excursion was the Maypole Festival on the town green (some form of ribbon-themed spring picnic, though of course there was dancing because this entire town still conspired to hurl potential brides at my brother).

With nothing to do but watch children attempt to tie each other in knots or eat over-stuffed cream cakes, Dido and I made an effort to draw the eldest Miss Bellamy into quiet conversation. It was not that we wished to get to know her better (hopefully we would never need to), but we did intend to demonstrate to Chambrey that we were not the snobs he imagined.

We spoke of gloves, and hats, and spring traditions and, of course, the conversation inevitably turned to our brother. This was quite the revelation.

There was no ambitious gleam in Miss Bellamy's eye when we mentioned Chambrey. She did not seize the opportunity to pump us for personal details of his tastes and preferences, as happened so often in the city. (Since he came into his fortune less than a year ago, the eligible misses had been circling like buzzards.) She did not tilt her head and sigh in any wistful way, as you might expect from any young lady whose head has been turned by a gentleman's attention.

Miss Bellamy was either the most politely discreet person I had ever met, or she genuinely had no romantic designs on my brother.

She spoke of the town, and how nice everyone was, and how she liked to dance, and how she liked to read a little, but mostly she preferred to hear one of her sisters read aloud while she did her sewing as it did not hurt her head…

Dido gave me a triumphant look over Miss Bellamy's bonnet. Her family might have made their fortune in blood and cruelty, but the eldest daughter appeared to be no genuine threat.

We were not out of the woods yet. Our brother might easily stumble into a permanent blunder — even if Miss Bellamy was not lovestruck enough to trap him, there was still that dreadful mother with golden guineas glowing in her eyes…

Still, we could be assured that once we finally dragged Chambrey away from the tiny town that never was, we would not be leaving a broken heart behind us.

Little did we know that a new threat would arise from a different member of her family.

From Miss Dimity Iverwold
to Miss Tatiana Rackham,
Malachite, Whistwipshire

My dear Tatiana,

As your brother will have informed you, we are settled at Elderflower Hall for the Season. I am bereft. Of course, you are not old enough yet to have properly enjoyed the fabulous sights and society of Abberline in spring. I look forward to introducing you to it all once you are Out in a few years.

Do not concern yourself that your brother will be too much the ogre in keeping you from the fun of city life — I know he is vigilant when it comes to your protection, but by the time you are Out I am sure to be married and terribly respectable, so I can bring you to all the best parties and displays. Now that Mr Rackham has seen how fiercely I defend my own brother against inappropriate courtships, I am sure he will trust me to take you about the place!

I rather envy you your army of governesses... if one must be trapped in the country, at least you are using your time to build your accomplishments and extend your education.

We have been entertained, here in Merrywist, by a series of assemblies at which my brother has become quite the centre of attention, as he is wont to do. As for your brother... well, you know I never gossip about Mr Rackham, as he is such a respectable gentleman and rarely makes any misstep worth crowing about. I hope you will not think badly of him to hear that he has quite offended the majority of society here in Merrywist — or at least, that portion of this rural society that despises gentlemen who are reluctant to run headlong into marriage.

This town teems with unmarried ladies (no eligible gentlemen to speak of at all, which can be the only expla-nation of how they can speak of nothing but the regiment coming to town next week!). Your brother has sensibly kept aloof, so as not to encourage any of the local young ladies.

One lady in particular — the sharp and forthright Miss Laura Bellamy — has created such a fuss. Several balls ago, my brother attempted with headstrong enthusiasm to persuade your brother to ask this lady to dance. Mr Rackham had no interest in doing so. Miss Laura somehow learned of this matter and has taken it as a personal slight, informing everyone in town that he is haughty and proud.

Why, at a recent town gathering on the green which I can describe only as The Ribboning (let us not inquire why any public event requires more than three maypoles), I overheard Miss Laura re-enacting the whole matter to her friends as a form of pantomime. The cheek of it!

Any sensible person would assume that after such an insult, Mr Rackham would be justified in having nothing more to do with this impertinent young lady.

And yet only an hour or so later, it happened again to the backdrop of a local brass band (dreadful) and the squeals of school children weaving maypole ribbons with sticky-fingered fervour. This time, the local squire presented Mr Rackham to Miss Laura, practically insisting that they dance for his amusement. (Is there a town conspiracy to match the pair? Some secret newspaper we do not receive.)

Mr Rackham conceded to the old fellow's demands, not being able to evade without being unforgivably rude. At which, that ~~hussy witch utterly ungrateful~~ lady had the gall to turn him down to his face.

Which would have been fine if not
If not
~~*How dare she laugh at*~~

No. Perhaps I would not write about the ribbon festivities to Tatiana. Alerting her to a pretty fortune hunter with fine eyes who might or might not be playing a dangerous game with Mr Rackham would only upset his sister, stuck as she was hundreds of miles away.

Tatiana could do nothing to save our gentlemen from making terrible mistakes. That was my task.

As I scrumpled up the letter I had been writing in the Elderflower Hall library, my thoughts drifted back to yesterday's awful ribbon fair, and what happened after Miss Laura Bellamy laughed off Mr Rackham's invitation...

"There you are," I said, approaching Mr Rackham from behind, as if I had only just spotted him, and not witnessed the Bellamy girl's latest attempt to humiliate him. Sir Willem, at least, had the grace to withdraw red-faced after causing this disaster.

Mr Rackham had not moved. He stood there with a rather strange look on his face as Miss Laura skipped away through the crowd.

"Ah, Dimity," he said as I rustled at his elbow. "Are you enjoying the revels?"

Oh, sarcasm, how I had missed you! "I have spent the last half hour being sweet and polite to Miss Bellamy," I informed him. "Only to discover that she is..."

"Genuinely insufferably nice?" He did not sound sarcastic this time, but his lips twitched with amusement.

"Yes!" I exclaimed. Finally, someone to share my frustration. "Even if she were a suitable match for Chambrey, we would have to put a stop to it. Any children born to that pair would be made of sugar and moonbeams, and would surely dissolve in the first shower of rain."

It was a relief to be around someone who did not look at you like a monster when you said unkind things. I thought of unkind things several times a day, and one can't always keep them on the inside without giving oneself a terrible stomach ache.

Mr Rackham's eyes were fastened thoughtfully on the distance, lost in thought. Miss Bellamy was no longer in sight, having dragged Miss Ellis off into a hedgerow somewhere.

Probably to relate with vengeful glee how she had cut a gentleman's pride to ribbons.

"What has you in such a reverie?" I asked, tapping Rackham on the arm with my pearl-tipped fan. "I hope you're not plotting vengeance against this dreary little town. That's *my* hobby. I suppose I might be willing to take you on as a henchman if you promise to supply me with a ready supply of re-usable witty insults..."

No one was better at sharply worded, clever drops of verbal poison than Mr Rackham. The society of Merry-wist was bound to have provided him with a great deal of inspiration.

"On the contrary," he said, blinking rapidly and offering me his arm so that we might perambulate together. "I was thinking of how pleasant it is when a lady does not hesitate to speak her mind. And if that confidence is matched with a pair of fine eyes..."

Dread sank into my pointy-toed shoes, but I covered it up with a merry laugh. "Oh, dear, Mr Rackham," I said in mock-pity. "Have you fallen under this township's spell as well as my brother? Which blood-stained Bellamy has caught your eye? You must tell me, so I can wish you joy in your future happiness."

Mr Rackham gave me a stern, half-amused look. "You ladies are so quick to leap to thoughts of matrimony," he rebuked me. "Most gentlemen hardly consider it at all. Your brother, for instance, is so determined to have a good time with his horses and hounds, I think he will not marry for another decade. And as for me..."

My breath caught a little. I had never seriously thought about Mr Rackham taking a wife, except for that brief whimsical time when I foolishly hoped he and Dido would fall madly & conveniently in love with each other. If he married, would we all still go about together in amiable company? Or would his wife have other ideas?

"No, it is quite settled in my mind," I said, continuing

the joke though it now felt rather ashen on my tongue. "What a mother-in-law you have chosen for yourself. I am sure Mrs Bellamy should move to Malachite with you at the drop of a hat to keep house…"

"And no one would be able to sleep for the sound of my father turning in his grave," said Rackham in a growl that was the closest he ever got to a laugh.

No, I would not write a word to Tatiana Rackham about Laura Bellamy and her fine eyes. It was a mere moment, a *nothing*, and I should not make more of it by setting it down on paper.

Mr Rackham was too sensible to fall in love with the wrong sort of lady. He was not the one I had to worry about.

I was sure of it.

CHAPTER 5
NO ONE EVER DIED OF A LITTLE COLD

"Miss Bellamy is coming to tea," said Dido, on a grey day with promise of showers.

I was so bored at this point, I almost welcomed it. "Only Miss Bellamy?"

"I was going riding," complained Chambrey, standing in the hall with his boots in one hand.

Dido gave him a sniff. "Ride if you like, brother. She's coming to tea with me and Dimity. Gentlemen are not essential."

I had not been informed until now of this engagement, but it did not surprise me. Dido had embarked on a new plot to make Miss Bellamy as tedious as possible to our brother, by befriending her with a fervour that was almost frightening.

Mr Harefield, not dressed for riding, looked from his wife to his brother-in-law and gave a loud sniff. "Looks like rain," he remarked, and disappeared into the library.

(Mr Harefield was not a great reader but no one could best him in a contest of sitting behind a newspaper and pretending he was interested in its contents.)

"Oh no!" declared Chambrey, packing his boots away and making for the stairs so as to change his clothes. "Mustn't be rude to guests!"

If Rackham had been there, he might have saved the situation by whisking Chambrey off into the damp fresh air, but he had been called back to the city for a few days on business.

From Miss Dimity Iverwold
to Miss Tatiana Rackham,
Malachite, Whistwipshire

Dear Tatiana

You would think that a town with no dragons to speak of would be free from the usual games of matchmaking and scheming — but Merrywist has once again surprised me.

Here, the mamas have to do all the hard work themselves, without elegant patrons or godmothers to arrange matters for them.

The more I hear of Mrs Bellamy of Longridge Grange,

the more I suspect she is a dragon in human form, or else she has one locked in her attic, giving her advice on the machinations of human courtship.

Surely no human would think enough steps ahead to send her daughter to tea on horseback in the <u>hope</u> it might rain, and then after said rain drenched the poor dear, to predict that we would not have a chaise to send her home, Mr Rackham having taken ours to the city.

What should have been a perfectly dull tea party, and a brief opportunity for my brother to make eyes at a young lady who shows only the slightest interest in anything he has to say, has now transformed into the world's awkwardest house party, with Miss Bellamy coughing daintily upstairs in a guest room.

Naturally with Dido and I both in residence, there is no chance of Miss Bellamy being compromised (much to the disappointment of the mama, I expect ~~ruthless harpy that she is~~!) but there is sadly far too much chance for Chambrey to compromise himself more deeply than the situation warrants.

~~I hope your brother returns to us soon, as I cannot take on the burden of sabotaging our house guest without his support.~~

We shall see what transpires and as always I will keep you up to date with our nonsense.

Your dear friend,

Dimity

MR RACKHAM RETURNED to Elderflower Hall the next morning, carrying a delicious scent of dragon smoke on his travelling coat as he shrugged it off at the door.

I bounded down several flights of stairs with far more energy than is strictly ladylike, and held back just in time from the kind of sisterly embrace I might have hurled at Chambrey.

Mr Rackham might be practically one of the family, but we still had to be mindful of my reputation.

I was about to interrogate him about his trip, when we were both subjected the bizarre appearance of Miss Laura Bellamy — flashing eyes, windswept hair, and six inches of mud on the hem of her dress — as she stormed up our open front door and came through it without ceremony or invitation.

"Miss Iverwold," she greeted me, ignoring Rackham, who looked as taken aback as I felt. "Will you please allow me to visit with my sister?"

I smiled my warmest smile, not wishing this untamed vixen to know that I recognised what a threat she was. "Of course, Miss Laura. Do come upstairs. I am sure dear Leda will be so surprised to see you."

(To my dismay, our recent tea had resulted in Miss Bellamy becoming 'dear Leda' to both Dido and I, before her sniffles overcame the allure of toasted muffins and butter and we were forced to send her to bed.)

Thank goodness I was wearing my newest morning dress; pale blue was terribly flattering on me, and the contrast between my assured elegance and Miss Laura's cavalier shabbiness gave me the strength to escort her to the sickroom.

Dido and Chambrey were both standing with Rackham in the hallway when I returned downstairs — Rackham's eyes swept over me as if checking for evidence I might have murdered our guest and tipped her body out a window.

"Was that Laura Bellamy?" Dido asked me in a hushed whisper.

I nodded, eyes wide. "Did you see her dress? I think she must have walked all the way."

Along muddy roads, at least two miles from Longridge, the morning after a heavy rainfall.

"Just when I think this town has a modicum of civilisation," Dido sighed.

"It shows a powerful family loyalty that Miss Laura cares more for her sister's health than for how she might appear to strangers," Chambrey said with a sunny smile.

Dido snorted. "Her health. What rot. No one ever died of a little cold."

I gave her an arch look to warn her that her game plan of agreeing with all of Chambrey's fancies was slipping. Dido gave me a snooty chin-tilt in turn, and hustled Chambrey back to the morning room.

"And you, Mr Rackham?" I said, returning my attention to our friend. "Has Miss Laura's exhibition of herself detracted at all from your admiration of a certain lady's fine eyes?"

Rackham gave me a look I rarely saw on his face — confusion, as if one of us was being entirely stupid. Then his expression cleared, replaced with its usual distant mockery. "On the contrary, Dimity," he said, with a curl of his lip. "They were brightened by the exercise."

Well, that was me told.

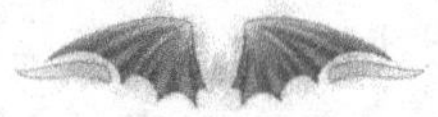

Miss Leda Bellamy caused little direct inconvenience to our household, as she remained in her room the entire time she was stricken by a cold.

Dido would not allow Chambrey to visit, or even to speak to dear Leda through the door, so that was all right.

Miss Laura, protective enough to kneel at her sister's door like a guard dog, was a greater problem.

Dido, in a surprising turn of agreeableness welcomed our guest downstairs, invited her to join us for meals, and generally threw a warm shawl of approval at the girl, for all the world as if she was ready to bind the Iverwolds and Bellamys together forevermore.

It was most discombobulating.

THAT FIRST EVENING, I hovered around Mr Rackham, grilling him about his visit to Abberline. He had been there at the same time as Lady Dorchester's pearl hunt *and* the Wyvern Gardens fireworks display, and I could not believe he had not condescended to witness even a crumb of the spectacles.

"I was there to see my banker," he was telling me when Miss Laura — all freshened up and disarmingly pretty in a borrowed dress of Dido's — slipped into the library. "I was not there to socialise, Miss Iverwold."

It was rare for him to 'Miss Iverwold' me at home; such was the sacrifice we made when entertaining strangers.

"You didn't go *anywhere* or see anything?" I lamented. Such a waste.

Rackham paused, giving Chambrey a chance to greet Miss Laura with a glass of port and lemon from the sideboard. "I may have taken a stroll through Hydde Park," he admitted in a low voice, not wanting my brother to hear.

I blinked a few times. "Oh." That was uncommonly nice of him. "I suppose..."

"I'm afraid not."

Of course not. If the Countess showed even a glimmer of jewel colour from beneath her granite grey,

Rackham would have told us immediately. He would not hesitate to share it with Chambrey and Dido if the news was *good*.

"Thank you," I murmured, eyes meeting his. "That was kind."

"I'm only sorry that..."

Oh, no, I would not accept pity. Everyone was turning back towards us, wondering what it was we had to talk about privately. "You really must write to Tatiana, Mr Rackham," I said in a louder voice, my usual teasing smile pasted on my face. "Tell her of your journey, and of the house, and the village..."

"What can I have to say to my sister that you have not written three times over?" he replied with an arch look.

"You could ask about her piano lessons," I said pointedly. "Give her a chance to boast a little."

Not that she would. Tatiana was the sweetest of us all, including even Chambrey. I understood why Rackham was so insistent on keeping her secluded in the country. If I could have built a tower for Chambrey and imprisoned him there until the age of thirty (or whenever he showed a strategic thought in his head, whichever came first) then I would not hesitate to do so.

"Claw!" exclaimed Dido, playing the charming hostess once again. "Shall we play?" She faltered almost immediately, realising that we were the wrong number for cards — even taking account that Mr Harefield did not care whether he played or not, Claw required only four players, not five.

"Please do not feel you need to entertain me," said Miss Laura with a gracious nod. "I can read a book."

What kind of books might appeal to a daughter of a hunter family? Adventure novels, probably. Blood and gore and battles.

"I'm afraid ours is a rather thin collection," said Chambrey with his usual affability, as if he knew anything at all about his new bookshelves. Why, he hadn't batted an eye when I devoted two days to reorganising every volume in this room by colour and then, two days after that, by category and author name.

It was not exactly that I had nothing to do in the country — but after a long winter of sewing and sketching and practicing the piano and reading, I was aching for culture, gossip and *parties*, not another three months of quiet pursuits.

The only thing worse than Merrywist's interminable round of country dances was the lack of them, and I had found myself rather at a loose end in Elderflower Hall this week.

Chambrey and Laura were still talking about books; that is to say, she mentioned several titles, about which he was terribly enthusiastic despite never having read them. It was painful to witness, but at least I didn't have to worry that *she* was going to inspire him into an unfortunate marriage — her eyes had that sort of polite sheen about them that people get when they wish that Chambrey would stop babbling.

He asked after the health of her sister no less than four times over the course of the evening, as if she was somehow able to divine the progression of Miss Leda's cough from several floors away.

Every time he did so, I gave Dido a pleading look. Surely she could see that this was getting out of control.

My sister gave me a stern shake of the head, as if I was the problem.

CHAPTER 6
ACCOMPLISHMENTS; PUNISHMENTS

Miss Laura Bellamy spent most of the next day in her sister's room. I suppose it was too much to hope she was busy denouncing my brother's potential as a future husband based on his inability to converse intelligently about modern authors.

It was raining again. I could not bring myself to embroider another scale on the tapestry cushion I was working on for Tatiana's birthday (several ruby-eyed dragon kits sprawled in a meadow, based on her favourite painting in the Willowisp Gallery) without hurling the thing against the wall.

Spring was for conversation and merriment and culture and longing to be invited to the next unmissable event. I simply did not know how to handle it in this backwater, where dance invitations had become some-thing to dread.

Perhaps I should learn another language. Or learn to ride. I'd never had the patience for the latter before because our previous country visits were full of amusements that did not require hovering several feet off the ground on a snorting creature that wanted you dead.

I spent the afternoon exploring the house. I'd found a Gothic novel squeezed between the philosophy tracts when re-organising the library, and while I would never read it *in front of anyone*, I was rather enjoying it as a bedtime treat. It was set in a castle, and the heroine Rhodella was convinced there was a secret dragon hidden somewhere in its walls, so she spent her nights wafting about in a long nightdress with a burning torch. Deliciously unseemly.

I wasn't prepared to go that far, but I was convinced Elderflower Hall had more secrets than it was letting on, and if that meant tapping various walls, flagstones and cupboards in the hope of finding a secret passage (Rhodella had already found six and I wasn't halfway through the book!) then it was not as if I had anything better to do.

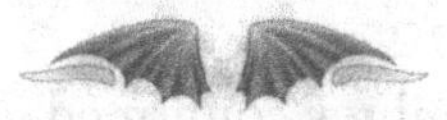

THAT NIGHT, after supper, which the Bellamy sisters had on trays in Leda's room, we all convened in the library. This time, Miss Laura finally condescended to join us.

I immediately bowed out of a round of Vault so that Dido could deal our guest in, along with Chambrey and Mr Harefield; Mr Rackham was finally writing a letter to his sister, and I did not want the Bellamy girl bothering him during this vital task.

Naturally, I bothered him instead.

"You must tell Tatiana about the maypoles."

"Yes, Dimity."

"And that ride you took to Selwyn's Bluff, I'm sure she'd love to hear about..."

Rackham's pen stilled. "Would you like to write this letter yourself, Dimity?"

I moved away with a small smile. "Not at all, I'm sure yours will be lovely. Such excellent penmanship."

"Better than mine," called out Chambrey from the card table.

I drifted towards the nearest bookcase, noticing that one of the volumes on ancient warfare was out of place. How had that happened? My fingers itched to fix it, without letting on that I felt remotely attached to this decrepit assortment of books. "A warthog with a fountain pen stuck through his nose would have better hand-writing than yours, dearest."

Miss Laura covered a laugh; I was annoyed, having forgotten her presence.

"It's true," Chambrey confirmed gravely, making Laura laugh out loud.

Drat. We were never going to be rid of her if we were merry *and* entertaining.

"We are all so fond of Mr Rackham's sister Tatiana," I announced, circling back towards him and the writing desk. "She's not Out, of course — still only sixteen." All of Laura's younger sisters were out, and at least one was younger than Tatiana. "She will dazzle Abberline once she finally debuts. Such an accomplished young lady, we will all be so proud to know her."

Rackham took this for the compliment it was, though he did not produce one of his rare smiles. "I do not require her to *dazzle*, as long as she is fully prepared for city society," he said seriously.

"Ladies are marvellous," declared Chambrey out of nowhere, causing Miss Laura to give him a very odd look.

Clearly, she was not yet used to Chambrey's random pronouncements — they generally made sense eventually, but one had to be patient until further context was provided.

"So *many* accomplishments," he rabbited on. "Every young lady I meet seems to be an expert in decorative arts. Covering screens, knitting socks for the poor, netting purses, painting tables and all that dainty stabbing with embroidery needles. Drawing and singing and cutting out finicky paper portraits..." He clearly recalled the winter I had practiced silhouetting, falling into a sort of fugue state for several months the year I turned eighteen. It had been an excellent method of channelling my nervous energy about being presented at court, whilst simultaneously terrifying my brother. "I shouldn't know how to do half of it." Chambrey had attempted handicrafts once or twice, but he is not a person designed to sit still with a pair of scissors. After three damaged tablecloths, Dido forbade him from further experiments.

Now Rackham did produce a smile: the tired sort that he generally brought forth when Chambrey was talking nonsense. (Or, perhaps, he was equally haunted by the memory of the Winter of Tiny Scissors.) "I think you'll find, Iverwold, that while ladies collectively may excel at all manner of artistry, there are very few individuals you could point to as fully accomplished."

True enough. Our standards, after all, were not defined by our fellow humans, but by the most exacting dragons of our acquaintance.

Laura laid down her cards, conceding the bout, and stood up from the table with fire in her eyes. "Is that so?"

"I agree," I said immediately. "Perhaps a dozen."

"Fewer," corrected Rackham.

"You don't attend as many sewing circles as I do," I reminded him.

"Having met my aunt, are you certain that is true?"

"Given that you both come from such a large and cosmopolitan city," purred Miss Laura, her eyes on Rackham rather than I. "You must know so many people. And yet, less than a dozen ladies meet your require-ments? That list of essential accomplishments must be very long indeed."

She sounded like she was mocking us. I could not imagine why. Rackham and I glanced at each other and nodded, in complete agreement.

Chambrey looked baffled. Dido was unreadable, though I could not imagine she approved of this exchange. Mr Harefield, freed from the obligation of the card table, made his escape to the rack of recent newspapers.

"May we all hear this list?" requested Miss Laura, her chin lifted in icy challenge.

"Handicrafts, of course," I replied immediately. "It pays to develop the skills to create two or three different kinds of decorative work to an exceptionally high standard. At the very least, one must demonstrate embroidery and ribbonwork for the everyday requirement of prettying up plain bonnets and pockets."

"Added to that," said Rackham, who would be the first to admit he knew little of sewing, though he had researched the art thoroughly in order to properly select Tatiana's governesses. "One would expect a lady to be trained in dancing, singing and a musical instrument."

"Modern languages," I put in. "A smattering of history and philosophy, so as to provide intelligent conversation..."

"Substance," added Rackham, his tone becoming softer. "Which is the hardest to learn from the schoolroom, though one may attain it through extensive reading..." I thought for a moment his eyes flickered in my direction, but no, that was intended as a complimentary nod to our guest. "A strong interest in attending museums and the theatre. The absorption and understanding of culture..."

"And grace in motion," I finished in triumph. "As expressed through a good walk, confidence in the dance, and the mastery of the perfect curtsey."

Mr Rackham nodded in approval. Taking custody of his much younger sister at an early age had been a source of great worry to him, and he had often consulted Dido — and, later, myself — on the less obvious but no less essential requirements of female education.

"Goodness," said Laura Bellamy, blinking at us both. "I am no longer surprised at you knowing only a dozen accomplished ladies. Do any exist? How are girls to find husbands, if this is the standard to which they are held in this city of yours?"

Now it was our turn to stare in surprise at her.

"Husbands," I repeated.

Laura's mouth twisted up as if she was not sure whether to laugh or pity me. "Is that not what all these accomplishments are *for*? Attracting gentlemen, like the bait on a hook?"

Humiliation washed over me in the face of her scorn.

"What an absurd idea," said Rackham, standing up all of a sudden. "Excuse me, all. I believe I will finish my letter in my room."

He held himself quite stiffly as he walked, which I knew meant he was angry.

Miss Laura stared after him, frowning a little. "I can't think why he took offence at that."

No, indeed. It was clear that *Mr Rackham* had not been the target at which she shot her arrow. Laura Bellamy was one of those young ladies who liked to tear other women down in order to make herself shine all the brighter.

"I think, Miss L," I said with my sweetest available smile. "You highly underestimate your ability to cause offence."

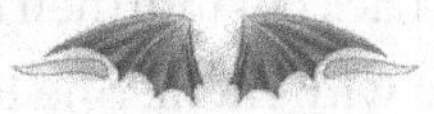

ON THE THIRD day of our invasion of the Bellamy sisters, a further incursion occurred. Mrs Bellamy, the honorary dragon, came calling upon us, all innocent concern as if enough time had passed that we might forget it was her machinations that gave dear Leda the cold in the first place.

She dragged her youngest daughter with her, not actually on leading strings (fifteen years old, I had learned from local gossip), but I was astonished to learn she was allowed to dance in public with gentlemen and not, for example, alongside the other children at the maypole.

Little Lavinia Bellamy had dark hair, bright eyes and a heart-shaped mouth. She was quite the silliest person I had ever met. Even her sister winced as Miss Lavinia bounced around our parlour, all ribbons and curls.

As soon as Chambrey greeted the new guests, the Bellamy matriarch took one arm and the precocious child took the other, and they overwhelmed him with compli-ments and giggles until he had agreed to host a ball here at Elderflower Hall, within the next fort-night.

I exchanged a pained glance with Laura, who seemed just as dismayed by this outcome as I — or perhaps, was embarrassed by the lack of subterfuge employed by her relations.

Having accomplished their goal, Mrs Bellamy and Little

Miss Lavinia swarmed upstairs to check on their poorly Leda, then swarmed back out into their carriage, and away.

Laura did not go with them. She looked unsettled, and I felt an odd sort of protectiveness, having seen a glimpse of her family life.

I still did not like her. How could I, when she was what she was?

However, I missed my friends, and Dido had been irritating me for days, and here was a perfectly well-read, intelligent young woman who would not leave our house as long as her sister continued ill.

"Do you want to look for secret passages with me?" I blurted out.

Laura Bellamy gave me an odd sort of smile. "You left that off your list of ladylike accomplishments."

I sighed in exasperation at her, as if she were one of my school chums. "Well, I haven't found one *yet*."

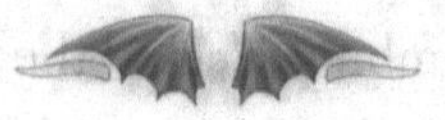

As it turned out, Laura Bellamy had also read *Nights in Castle Dread*, and had many opinions about our heroine Rhodella that were wrong-headed enough that we could cheerfully bicker about it for hours.

Exactly at the moment I thought we had survived the day without some kind of dreadful conversation, she cleared her throat.

"Miss Iverwold, may I ask you what it was I said last night that was so very... unfortunate?"

I sighed. We still had three walls of the attic to examine, but clearly she had other priorities.

"I am not suggesting I was gentle in my speech," Laura went on. "But given that the entire direction of the conversation about Mr Rackham's perfect sister and the accomplishments of ladies felt designed as an insult towards myself and my family, I am not sure how it is that I was left with..."

"Blood on your hands?" I said sharply.

"In a manner of speaking."

The truth was, I did not know why her barb had stung Mr Rackham as sharply as it had. There were times he was an open book to me, and other times parts of his life and thoughts were walled off entirely.

He rarely seemed concerned by the matter of marriage. Perhaps it was because we had brought Tatiana into the conversation. I knew he was sensitive about the responsibility that came with preparing her for future marriage. I did not wish to assume his anger stemmed from any deeper feeling towards Miss Laura, but that did not mean it could not be true.

"Your family and ours are from different worlds," I said finally.

"I know that," Laura said, with some of the familiar scorn. "You and Mr Rackham have communicated quite effectively that anything amusing to the people of Merrywist is a punishment to you both."

Accurate, and fair. Still, it barely grasped at the full story.

"Mr Rackham's family and my own are part of Abberline society. To be one of the Nine Hundred... invited to great houses, included in the Season... is a privilege. One that can never be taken for granted."

I had learned that the hard way. The Iverwold family was far too new for some society families to tolerate, no matter how well my Papa and Grandfather had married up. It might have been different if the Countess remained in our corner, but by the time I started school, it was already known that our dragon had been sleeping for several seasons.

There is no group quite as snobbish as a gaggle of twelve-year-old girls who have been taught to be impressed by the superiority of their families. I was lucky to eventually find a few good friends who could overlook that my grandfather had been in trade.

Laura frowned; I had not explained myself sufficiently to her yet.

"The artistry, making pretty things, the poise and grace, the singing and dancing," I said, somehow desperate to make her understand — to say aloud the knowledge that I lived with, always. "All those accomplishments expected of ladies, especially the unmarried. None of it is for the benefit of *gentlemen*. Do you think Chambrey would care a jot if a lady he liked was able to arrange flowers or play the harpsichord or provide expert botanical sketches, while discussing the latest novels by Brecker or Normany?"

Laura bit her lip, a terrible habit. If she had a dragon in the family, she would have been trained by now to avoid such childish mistakes. "I think perhaps," she said thoughtfully. "That as long as the lady was kind, and had a pretty face, and liked dogs and horses, Mr Iverwold would not mind whether she knew how to sing arias or play the nose flute. Having discussed novels with him myself, I rather think that holding opinions on authors would be more of a flaw than an ornament."

"I see you have the measure of my brother," I said, with a reluctant smirk. "Accomplishments aren't to please potential husbands, Miss Laura. They're to please the dragons."

She let out a low hiss. "The dragons?"

"Of course. A lady's reputation rises and falls on what the dragons think of her. There are balls and assembly halls and tea parties to which one would never be invited without the kind condescension of..."

"So, it's not about *marriage*?"

"It's always about marriage," I conceded. "No one in Abberline would dare marry without the approval of her family's dragon, and that of her preferred spouse... but it's more than that. The best matches are made by the dragons, not by human families. Surely it's the same in the country."

Not here; obviously not in Merrywist, where there were hardly any dragons to be seen. But Mr Rackham's terrifying Aunt Beautrice commanded half of Whistwipshire, and many of the more powerful godparents and matriarchs had a country seat to tyrannise as well as a townhouse.

Perhaps hunter families simply did not mind so much what dragons thought of them, because they were too busy planning to stab them in the belly.

Laura Bellamy's mouth was a thin line. "Why is it only the ladies who must perform for the approval of these scaled patrons?"

"It is not so," I argued. "We were speaking of ladies last night, but the human gentlemen must prove their worth in all manner of ways — athletic prowess, courtesy and refined manners, tailoring. They are judged down to the same intricate detail as the ladies. And while they might not be expected to play the harpsichord or hand-stitch a meadow of flowers, there is one measure to which they must always come up to scratch."

"Their fortune," said Laura, in a voice lacking tone.

"Their hoard," I corrected gently. "And their ability to guard it from the outside world."

"You have given me much to think about, Miss Iverwold," murmured my new friend.

"Call me Dimity," I invited her.

I DON'T KNOW who was more alarmed to discover at supper that I had befriended Laura Bellamy: Chambrey,

Dido or Mr Rackham. They eyed us with suspicion, as if I was about to poison my new friend's soup.

After supper, as it was still raining outside, I invited Laura to take a turn about the library with me; while its scooped ceilings lacked the grandeur of Mr Rackham's family library, in which one could host twelve couples dancing if one wished, the Elderflower Hall library still had suitable proportions to allow for some exercise without making ourselves dizzy.

Mr Rackham glanced up from his book as we swept past him, and I invited him to join us in our stroll.

"No, indeed," he said, with an oddly whimsical look in his eye. "I can fathom only two reasons for your chusing to circle our perimeter, and my inclusion could only interfere."

If I had been holding a fan, I would have swatted it at him. "What can he mean?"

"Do not ask him to expound," said Laura, squeezing my arm. "Think how disappointed he shall be."

I gave Mr Rackham a severe glare. Never had a man looked so entirely innocent.

"No," I said, after we had circled the library once. "I must know. What two reasons do you think we have for walking thus?"

Rackham shrugged, setting his book aside. "Either you have secret matters to discuss, or you think your figures appear to the greatest advantage while walking. If the former, I should be entirely in the way, and if the latter... I can admire you better from here."

For several heartbeats, I was lost for words. Mr

Rackham was always such a gentleman. He had never said anything so flirtatious to me in his life.

Of course, I was not the object of his address.

"Abominable," I said finally, with a toss of my head, when I had recovered my sensibilities. "How shall we punish him, Laura?"

"Oh, no," said Laura, going so far as to let out a low laugh, turning into my shoulder so as to conceal it. "Not I, Dimity. I shall leave that duty entirely to you.

CHAPTER 7

ON THE FLATTERING EFFECT OF FLAMECOATS, AND OTHER UNFORTUNATE REVELATIONS

The militia had arrived at Merrywist, which demoted our household from the top of the list of alluring novelties. Given the lack of convenient dance partners at the rural assemblies, it was hardly surprising that the flash of gold-trimmed flamecoats had the locals in a tizzy.

One heard of nothing else at the milliner's but that the fine young men had been strolling up and down the local streets, and the Colonel had a pretty wife who had promised dinners to all the fine families, and so on, and so forth.

"If we can't have dragons," remarked Miss Ellis with a wistful smile. "At least we have peacocks, do we not?"

My friendship with Miss Laura Bellamy had waned somewhat, since she swept her sister back home (to the great dismay of her scheming mama). I had therefore turned my attentions back to Miss Allicot Ellis, whose potential as an amiable companion was greatly enhanced by her lack of romantic ambition.

One must have someone on one's arm if one is to peruse ribbons without buying them, one of the only pleasant activities available in Merrywist. Miss Ellis was amusing enough for the task.

It also did not hurt to have a local guide who could murmur telling details in my ear when we crossed paths with our neighbours. I had collected quite the repository of gossip with which to regale Dido over tea.

As we emerged from the lending library (which was, like Elderflower Hall's library, entirely lacking in history of the [Something]—shire families and their dragons), Miss Ellis and I beheld such a fascinating scene that we both paused behind our parasols.

In the cobbled street, right at the turn from the first shopping avenue into the second, all five of the Bellamy sisters were arrayed in cream muslin and freshly trimmed bonnets. They were accompanied by a round little clergy-man, who hopped about with excitement as if he were on the pantomime stage. He talked with his hands and feet, which made for quite the show.

Two soldiers, dashing in their flamecoats and hats, had accosted the ladies in order to display their ~~feathers~~ charm, and were being charmed in return (how the hunters and the prey circle each other in small towns!) with such a fluttering of fans, swinging of reticules and heaving of bosoms that it was astounding any of them had sufficient oxygen to continue.

"Oh, my," said Miss Ellis, entirely intrigued.

I longed for further (detailed!) commentary from my companion as to what she made of this scene, but that would have to wait. The sound of hooves filled the air, and two gentlemen — my *own* gentlemen, as it happened — rode towards the gathering.

Chambrey arrowed in on Miss Bellamy the elder as if she were the only person in the world. We really were going to have to do something about that; he was entirely too forward. Not only his heart, but also his stomach and kidneys were pinned to his sleeve, while the lady in question remained only mildly encouraging. Such behaviour would end either in marriage or my brother making a fool of himself, and I could not abide either option.

Mr Rackham, world-weary in Chambrey's shadow, remained in the saddle even as my brother hurled himself to the ground and made friendly conversation with the group.

From our position halfway down the street, I heard the name "Mr Rackham!" bellowed with enthusiasm by the round little clergyman, who capered forth to get his attention, apparently delivering some kind of pompous speech.

I do enjoy watching Mr Rackham's personal struggle with being polite to strangers, and so my attention was on him when his eye fell upon one of the soldiers.

Rackham froze, his entire countenance becoming so politely unassuming that he might have transformed himself into a hat-rack.

The soldier looked surprised but not displeased to see Mr Rackham. Holding his gaze, he bowed.

Mr Rackham turned his horse and rode away without a word, practically covering the poor little clergyman in dust.

"Goodness!" gasped Miss Ellis beside me.

Goodness, indeed.

Now that Mr Rackham had made his exit, I turned my attention to the soldier whose presence had so surprised him. He was a tall fellow, with reddish gold hair, and a handsome if rather pointed face. This combined with the coppery tones of the flamecoat uniform, gave him the appearance of a storybook fox or perhaps one of those dragon riders in the more romantic portraits.

There was something familiar about him, but I could not imagine where our paths might have crossed. I do not make a habit of giving the time of day to soldiers, unless social obligation dictates it, and the drawing rooms of Abberline are hardly the place for roving militia.

While the Bellamys flapped about the soldier with their ribbons and reticules, taking noisy offence on his behalf at Mr Rackham's rudeness, the soldier himself did not seem remotely distressed.

If anything, he seemed remarkably pleased with himself.

"Who was that soldier in the street today?" I asked Mr Rackham later, shortly before we went into supper.

A torn expression crossed his face. "That man is Gideon Fairbanks."

"Oh!" No wonder he had seemed familiar, though I had not set eyes on the fellow in a decade or more. "That boy from your estate. He pushed me in the river!"

Caught off guard, Mr Rackham laughed. "Of course you remember that."

I was only five, but that sort of memory stays with you. Young Rackham had boxed the lad's ears for it, which led me to think of him as a white knight for ages afterwards, though Chambrey told me that Rackham only did it to prevent me biting the boy in the leg.

"Never doubt my ability to hold a grudge," I said archly, leaving aside the matter of who had avenged whose honour. "Wasn't he the son of your father's gamekeeper?"

"The steward."

"I remember your father paid for his schooling!" My father had not approved — called it a weakness, to give advantages to the undeserving, and so on. Which explains rather why my father always struggled to keep good servants. "You used to be such chums, didn't you?"

"Not for a very long time," Mr Rackham said, looking grave.

"That was obvious today! Whatever did he do to earn your enmity?"

I have known Mr Rackham to dislike many people,

but it is rare for his friendship, once given, to be so whole-heartedly removed.

He looked for a moment as if he wanted to tell me, then shook his head. "It is a matter of honour. I cannot share the details."

"Then do not, by all means." I might be a devoted gossip, but I wasn't a sneak. Everyone deserved their secrets. "I shall not ask if it pains you..." I would simply assume whatever Mr Fairbanks had done was at least as bad as pushing a tiny girl in the river and proceed accordingly.

"Wait," Rackham said, sounding a little hoarse. His hand brushed against mine; it was rare for him to make such intimate gestures. "Dimity. Do you trust me?"

"Always," I said immediately. Outside my own family, he was the person I trusted most in the world.

Mr Rackham was usually so poised; when he did lose control of his countenance it was to grumpiness or quiet rage rather than this strange sort of sadness. I had not seen him so lost since the funeral of old Mr Rackham.

He moved his hand away. "Dimity, all you need to know about Mr Gideon Fairbanks is that you cannot trust one word that comes out of his mouth. Please keep that in mind, should you become acquainted again."

"I am sure we shall not," I said. "The militia are hardly of any interest to me, though I suppose we must have them to the ball." Chambrey had become bosom brothers with half the regiment already, and there would be a scarcity of dance partners without them.

"And perhaps," said Rackham, speaking with care.

"You might ensure that any young ladies of your acquaintance are likewise warned? Gently, with all due discretion."

Oh. There was that sinking feeling again. "You mean Miss Laura, I suppose?" I had seen her today, tipping her smiles up at the handsome soldier, every bit as brazen as her younger, sillier sisters.

Still foremost in Mr Rackham's thoughts.

"I'm sure it is nothing to worry about," he said, reaching out as if to touch my hand again, but drawing back just in time. He spun around and left the room.

"Mr Rackham," Dido called out to him. "Are you not joining us for supper?"

Our friend was already up the stairs and away, lost in his own thoughts.

Taking all my best gossip from the day with him.

CHAPTER 8
BOILING POINT AT THE ELDERFLOWER BALL

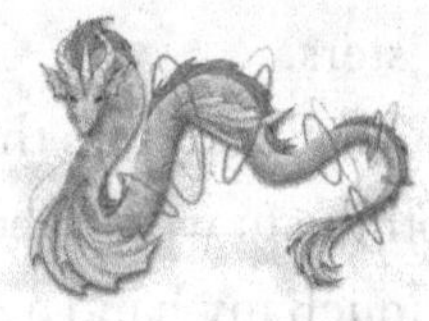

It was an odd sort of thing, to prepare for a ball without dragons to please.

We Iverwolds have not had our own patroness looking over our shoulder for years, but when we have hosted events — that is to say, when Dido has hosted events, with me doing all of the tasks she cannot abide — it is rarely without the oversight or consideration of dragons.

Depending on who is invited, where one has been invited lately, and which dragon of the Coterie might be taking a particular interest in one's endeavours, planning something as important as a society ball usually means that the tastes and refined preferences of at least six dragons loom over one's preparations.

If poached meringues are to be served at Mrs Walpole's soiree next week, then one cannot *also* serve poached meringues, unless Mrs Devonthwait has come out of hibernation and is on the guest list, in which case, one must *only* serve poached meringues.

The Duchess of Wildfell prefers a ballroom to be illuminated by candlelight, which should not matter as she will not attend your ball, but if her great-nephews are on the guest list, it is better to be safe than sorry, or one will never hear the end of it.

The Marchioness of Grimsdyke will lecture everyone in the Nine Hundred on the gentle delicacy of paper lanterns, but only in shades of lavender or azure, if any of her god-daughters are likely to dance.

If the Highwaters are invited then extra grilled meat must be prepared in the kitchens for the chances of their Great Aunt Edith making a surprise visit are exceedingly high and woe betide any hostess who does not have a platter of tidbits waiting for her.

All of this tension and drama was entirely absent from our preparations for the first ball at Elderflower Hall. There was no challenge to it. No limit. No threat of social ruin at every turn.

Somehow, even with Dido heaping most of the work on my shoulders, it managed to be exceedingly dull.

As I refined the refreshments plan, and the decorations order, and the set list for the string quartet, I occasionally found myself seeking out Mr Rackham in the library or the garden to ask whether the esteemed Lady Beautrice de Bramble had a preference between cold ham or cold tongue, or an opinion on mulligatawny soup, or a stance on paper lanterns.

Finally, he pushed back from his newspaper and gave

me a weary but knowing sort of look— the kind of look that goes right through you, to the bone. "You are aware that my aunt is not attending this ball, Miss Iverwold?"

I blinked at him. "I... of course, I know that. Though she would be more than welcome."

No, Dimity, one does not invite the majestic Lady Beautrice de Bramble to travel across several counties in order to attend a rural ball. What had I been thinking?

Rackham gave a low laugh that somehow did not make me feel entirely mocked. "You are good at this, Dimity," he informed me. "Trust your own taste. It is generally excellent, and you will rarely be given opportunity to prove it until you are married."

I huffed at him, though secretly pleased at his endorsement. "Just for that, I'm ordering the pink lanterns *and* the green candles."

"Oh, no," he rumbled, returning to the newspaper. "However shall I survive such a punishment."

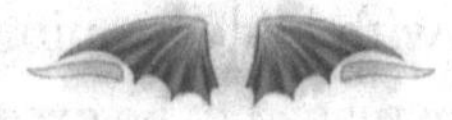

WHEN MISS ELLIS arrived on the morning of the ball to help me arrange the flowers (I had no need of the assistance, but was so starved for entertainment I was actually craving updates on town gossip), I found her bursting with news.

"Do you know Mr Muggins?" she asked me.

I did not.

"He is a cousin of the Bellamys, visiting from Wutheringshire. A clergyman."

"Oh, that chatty little man in the street," I remembered. "Rather shaped like an egg."

"That's the one." Her eyes were oddly bright. "You see, he's the heir of Mr Bellamy's estate."

"An entail? How barbaric." Not that my father would not have tied twenty entails around his fortune with red ribbons if he could, so determined was he to leave everything to his son and nothing to his daughters.

No wonder Mrs Bellamy had such an air of desperation, with five daughters to settle and no home to fall back on, should they fail to marry to advantage. She must hear a ticking clock every time she passed her silver-haired husband in the passageway.

Miss Ellis nodded. "His patroness told him, Mr Muggins that is, that he ought to make things right by offering marriage to one of his cousins."

"Unsurprising."

"He wanted Leda..."

The eldest and prettiest, of course. That would certainly solve a problem for us. "She would not have him?"

"He was dissuaded from asking." Miss Ellis looked somewhat embarrassed. Of course, the mama had her eye on Mr Chambrey Iverwold with his five thousand a year for her eldest. She would not waste Leda's potential on a mere curate even to save the family home. "His eye has now fallen on *Laura*."

"Oh!" That would be a blow for Rackham, if Miss

Laura's fine eyes were swept out of reach. But would she accept the offer? I could not imagine a worse candidate for a curate's wife. I might have accidentally become friends with that young lady thanks to our mutual love of gothic literature, but it was clear from our short acquaintance that she was far too tactless and animated for a life of public service. "That will offer some entertainment for the ball," I said without thinking.

Miss Ellis looked at me, horrified, and then burst into giggles. "She doesn't want him. Not at all. But her mama…"

We both took a moment of silence to thank the heavens that neither of us had been born with Laura Bellamy's mama.

As IT TURNED OUT, it did not matter whether the flower arrangements were perfect, the lanterns were tasteful, or the quadrilles outnumbered the cotillions.

The ball was always going to be a disaster.

It was also the best thing that could possibly have happened to the Iverwold family.

I had, I must admit, forgotten entirely about Gideon Fairbanks despite my promise to Mr Rackham.

As our guests arrived, greeted with such effusiveness from Chambrey that one might think each of them were individually his best friend in the world, it became quickly apparent that Mr Fairbanks had chosen the path of least resistance. Rather than confront whatever bad feeling lay between himself and Mr Rackham, he had elected to excuse himself entirely.

It started well. The ballroom was exquisite, decorated with paper lanterns depicting famous dragons from history; we had opened the doors to the terrace, displaying the beauty of the Elderflower Hall grounds, and allowing the gentle spring breeze to circulate in the room. The people of Merrywist were eager to see the house again after so many years without a tenant in place to invite them. Chambrey had arranged entertainments in the garden: fire jugglers, a floral swing, and a carousel for the children before it grew dark.

Nothing too outrageous by Abberline standards, but clearly a little *more* than this town usually enjoyed.

The militia themselves, in their formal flamecoats and golden braid, were the hit of the party, offering willing dance partners for the starved young ladies of the town.

Even Mr Rackham, once he realised his old nemesis had not graced us with his presence, joined in the hosting duties, leading the dance with Dido on his arm.

The Bellamy family were in their full finery, as I suppose must have seemed appropriate for so splendid a ball; this meant that we were once more forced to endure the jewelback tiara, the hydra-eye locket, the opaltooth pearls and the wyvern skin purse.

I did my best to avoid looking at the dreadful little

blood trophies, which meant that I took far too long to notice that Miss Laura was on the war path.

Dear Leda, by contrast, greeted me with her usual restrained friendliness, which I was able to meet with similar grace by keeping my gaze below her hairline, so I did not have to look at the tiara.

"This is a lovely ball," Leda assured me, still pink in the face from having danced her pair with Chambrey at the top of the ball (while her sister Laura suffered the same at the hands of the awkward Mr Muggins). "You and Mrs Harefield are to be commended."

"That is sweet of you to say," I replied, which was true; every other young lady had credited Chambrey for hosting the event, rather than thinking to compliment those who did the work.

"You must not worry about Laura," Leda added, and then blushed slightly, as if she had said too much.

Until this moment I had not had the slightest worry about Laura. Now, I glanced around the ballroom and while my eye did not land immediately on the second (and most troublesome) Bellamy sister, I did see *something*.

People were talking.

It is of course expected that guests at a ball will talk among themselves, but there is talk and talk. Once you have attended enough assemblies (and I was still, at the age of nearly two-and-twenty, a mere novice by comparison to the grand ladies of Abberline) you can tell when a piece of gossip has reached boiling point.

The Countess, when she was awake and gracious

enough to share her wisdom about society with the Iverwold family, used to say that gossip was like music. One could feel the vibrations of it on the air, not only in the words whispered in cutting undertones, but in the way eyes darted about when a juicy story was shared, the intake of breath, the curling smile of astonishment.

I felt it now, the ripple of it. Soldiers and young ladies alike were gossiping like mad, and every single one of them had their eyes fixed upon Mr Rackham.

Mr Rackham, who was at this very moment bowing before Laura Bellamy. After a frozen moment in which the entire ballroom stared at them, she accepted his invitation to join the next dance.

The music was pleasant, the dancing exquisite, and any other hostess might have thought this a crowning moment of her evening. I stood there, watching, as Laura Bellamy made a remark to Mr Rackham. He replied, looking confused in the first instance, then immediately thunderous.

"What has she done?" I breathed.

"Laura never means any harm," said dear Leda, in the practiced tones of one who has had to repeat that phrase many times in her life. "It is only that she was so disappointed not to see Mr Fairbanks at the ball tonight."

Now it was my breath that gave a sharp intake. "He did not chuse to accept our invitation," I said.

Mr Rackham and Miss Laura Bellamy continued to dance, and speak, and it was by far the worst thing I had ever seen. Her disdain for him was clear in every gesture, every toss of her head, while he went from furious to something very like hurt, and back again.

I wanted to stab her in the neck.

"Oh," said Leda, surprised to hear that it was Mr Fairbanks who had chosen to stay away. "She thought perhaps Mr Rackham had insisted... in any case, she has become rather fond of Mr Fairbanks. Nothing inappropriate, but they have made a fast friendship, and she was hoping to dance with him tonight." *Instead of Mr Muggins,* I imagined, remembering Laura's sour face as the two of them stumbled through the first pair of dances. *Instead of Mr Rackham,* currently being tortured in the arms of a young lady with ribbon roses on her slippers. Leda continued to explain, every detail making it worse: "Mr Fairbanks has, in the course of their new friendship, told Laura a great many things about Mr Rackham's treatment of him in the past. Her sympathy is entirely with that other gentleman."

Pretty Mr Fairbanks, whose presence in the village made Mr Rackham pale with fury; I should have enquired further. If honour prevented him from explaining what had happened, then surely Dido or Chambrey knew something. All of my protective instincts rose, reminding me of what I had said to my sister before this whole terrible endeavour began: *I wish I were a dragon.*

For a start, Laura Bellamy would no longer have eyebrows.

"Your sister has shared these stories, I imagine, with a

select few intimates?" I inquired, my tone veering towards the dangerously vexed.

"Yes, indeed," Leda said quickly. "Only... that does include all of our sisters."

The sisters who were currently cuddled up to the soldiers, flirting and laughing and whispering in their ears. No wonder the gossip had spread so quickly. Mr Fairbanks did not have to attend the ball in order to ruin it; he needed only to tell his tale of woe to Miss Laura and encourage her to light the touch paper for him.

Rage burned behind my eyes. If I had the breath of flame, there would be no Bellamys left on the face of the earth, except perhaps the one standing next to me.

I squeezed her hand impulsively, not wanting her to know how angry I felt. "You are a good friend, Leda. Thank you for letting me know."

"I would have not said anything," that lady assured me. "If not that when I mentioned the matter to Mr Iverwold during our pair, he assured me that while he knew none of the particulars of why Mr Rackham and Mr Fairbanks had fallen out so many years ago, he would personally vouch for his friend's good conduct, probity and honour above all things."

"Yes," I said softly. "That is perhaps the wisest thing my brother has ever said." Chambrey always believes the best in people, and yet if pressed I must admit that when it comes to selecting those people in whom he believes more than anyone else, he has chosen well.

It was possible I had not been giving him enough

credit that he would use the same measure when selecting a wife.

Across the room, I saw Chambrey and Dido in amiable conversation, completely unaware of the venomous melody being played from one end of the ballroom to the other.

I stood still and quiet, watching from the sidelines as Mr Rackham and Miss Laura danced together. Finally, the excruciating ordeal was over; he bowed with gritted teeth and waited for the string quartet to begin again.

Laura had already turned with one last toss of her head, leaving him on the dance floor with one dance of their pair unfinished. She walked straight out on the terrace and away; the snub could not be more evident.

Mr Rackham immediately withdrew himself, speaking briefly to Dido before disappearing into the house, away from the prying eyes in the ballroom.

"Please excuse me, dear Leda," I said, with as much politeness as I could muster. "I would speak with my sister."

This was a lie, of course, but I considered it entirely justified. If I had spoken the truth, it would only have alarmed the sweetest young lady in Merrywist. *Please excuse me. I must eviscerate your sister.*

I walked through the crowd in Dido's direction, then swerved at the last minute to head out through the terrace doors.

Miss Laura Bellamy had some explaining to do.

CHAPTER 9
WHAT HAPPENS IN THE GREENHOUSE STAYS IN THE GREENHOUSE

I found Miss Laura Bellamy hiding from Mr Muggins. At least, I assumed this was her motivation, given that I had spotted that gentleman moments earlier, wandering the grounds with two glasses of cucumber sorbet, searching in vain for his future wife.

"I believe she may be found in the library," I informed him, my eye falling on a pair of dancing slippers that had been abandoned near the greenhouse door. They had bright green shoe-roses on them and were last seen marching away from Mr Rackham.

Mr Muggins went one way; I went the other.

The Elderflower Hall greenhouse was majestic; I still believed that it was, like the greenhouse belonging to the Ellis family nearby, originally designed for a dragon to hibernate here. Why else would the plants themselves be relegated to the edges of the space, leaving a large expanse of paving in the centre.

The pillars were basalt, a dark and elegant greenish-black stone which might look rather gloomy were it not for the enormous arches and many glass panes of the pavilion, tinted to cast a somewhat eldritch sunlight over the plants during the day, and create ominous moonshine shadows at night.

There was room for two dragons the size of the Countess to curl up together, surrounded by hothouse flowers and tomato plants, if that was their desire.

There were sculptures everywhere, all botanical in design: roses, pineapples, hydrangeas and cornucopias, depicted in that same basalt. Not a single dragon statue in sight; which was for the best, otherwise I should have spent weeks obsessing over whether it was a real dragon likely to awaken.

It would have been quite dark in here as I entered, but I had the forethought to bring a paper lantern with me; this one was lavender, shaped like the legendary Hydra, with a candle burning at its centre and many fluttering paper heads on all sides.

Laura Bellamy sat on a wide stone bench at the far end of the greenhouse, underneath a bower of carved basalt strawberries. Her feet were bare and her expression somehow both pensive and cross at the same time. Her head came up with a jolt as I approached; I was still wearing shoes, and they clicked against the warm paving stones.

"Miss Laura," I said, pasting a smile upon my face as I approached, and selecting my greeting to make it very clear that we were no longer friends. "I hear you are delighted with Gideon Fairbanks! Such a handsome gentleman, so charming, and so full of stories about his deprived childhood."

On my way across the terrace I had overheard little Lavinia Bellamy, the youngest of the vipers, telling the impressionable Sophiar Ellis how the swoony Mr Fairbanks had been shamefully deprived of his inheritance from Mr Rackham's late father, thanks to the son's jealousy. Three steps across the lawn at the floral swing, I had heard Lottie Bellamy sharing the same story with several equally credulous gentlemen of the militia.

Laura Bellamy narrowed her eyes at me. "I suppose you are going to tell me that you know all about it," she said.

"On the contrary. I haven't the least idea of the particulars. But I may surely hold an opinion on how inappropriate it is to spread another person's spite on their behalf."

"Indeed," said Laura, all icy disdain. "If only Mr Fairbanks were allowed to cross your threshold, he might have spoken for himself."

I laughed at that; I couldn't help myself. "The man isn't dead, Miss Laura. Merely chose to absent himself of your company for one evening, so he might not face the man he has maligned behind his back."

"How clever you are," said Laura smoothly. "To be so well-informed on a matter when you haven't the least idea of the particulars."

"I know Mr Rackham is an honourable man. That you should take the word of some steward's son against him..."

"Ah!" she exclaimed; and rightly so. I had let myself down there. "And you would happily hear testimony against Mr Rackham if it came from a higher born gentleman, would you? Rather than the son of a steward."

"I have nothing against sons of stewards in general," I said between gritted teeth. "But given that this particular son of a steward pushed me in a river when I was five years old, you will allow me to deny him the benefit of the doubt!"

"I'd like to push you in a river," grouched the lady, if that term could still be said to apply.

"Indeed," I said, my voice rising slightly above the bounds of politeness. "If you persist in speaking ill against my brother's dearest friend, I'm afraid you shall have to leave."

Laura leaped to her feet. "It is astonishing to me that your brother is so amiable and charming, when the rest of your household is so objectionable."

I was ready to throw something at her head; it might have been a potted tomato plant or, if nothing else was within range, my own shoes from my feet. Instead, my hand closed around an enormous basalt pinecone, which — had it come free of its plinth — would have surely knocked Miss Laura Bellamy into next week.

Instead, when I tugged on the stone pinecone, there was a grinding, shifting sound, and the stone pavings opened up beneath her. Miss Laura disappeared into the darkness with a scream; I had found my secret passage at last.

THE STAIRCASE WAS RATHER PRETTY; a shame it was largely hidden by design. Each step was wide and shallow, with a slightly different dragon scale pattern; at the foot of this staircase designed for dragons to use, a dark passage curved off into the distance, wide and tall.

(The perfect hiding place for a dragon's hoard, if one's family had both dragon and hoard in need of such arrangements.)

Also at the foot of the stairs: Miss Laura Bellamy, who had by great fortune and a well-padded ballgown, entirely failed to break her leg.

Or her neck. But she was clutching her ankle as if it pained her, so that had likely been the greater danger.

"I told you so," I said, as my paper lantern with its many Hydra heads illuminated her face in shades of lavender. "Secret passage."

She stared at me, and then let out a sound that was probably a laugh (though not entirely ladylike). "You do like to be right, don't you, Dimity?"

"It is one of my favourite pastimes. Did you hurt yourself?"

Laura attempted to rise, made a small sound, and sagged down again. "I don't think it's broken. But I need assistance."

"I'm sure you do." I sat neatly on the stairs, smoothing

out the silk of my ballgown. "I shall of course be glad to help you out of here... once you vow to apologise."

"Apologise?" Her cheeks had taken on the shade of a rich plum in the lavender light. "Apologise for telling the truth?"

"Apologise for spreading lies about a friend of this household."

"You're certain, are you, that Mr Fairbanks speaks untruths?"

"I am certain that Mr Rackham does not. He bade me warn you, you know. That Mr Fairbanks was not a trust-worthy gentleman."

"Of course he did. Mr Fairbanks is not one of us, is he? He does not belong to the illustrious and graceful Nine Hundred. You don't even know his story!"

I had heard enough of it for one night. "I do not wish to."

"How Mr Rackham senior took an interest in the boy, paid for his schooling, had such plans for his future... did you know it was an old tradition, even in Hoarding fami-lies, that a second son would be apprenticed to Hunters?"

A very old tradition indeed, and one most families would not consider now. "Mr Fairbanks wished to be a dragon hunter?" No wonder Mr Rackham despised him; no wonder the Bellamys took his side. "Mr Fairbanks was not Mr Rackham's son," I added quickly. "Second or otherwise."

"He wrote into his will that Mr Fairbanks should have a sponsored living," Laura said, her eyes sparkling with spite. "But he died while the boys were still at school, and when it came time for Mr Fairbanks to make his way in the world, Mr Rackham cut him off without a penny."

"I do not believe he would do that," I replied without a moment's hesitation.

"You do not believe that a man so proud of his heritage as Mr Rackham might well deny a future dragon hunter his living?"

She could not shake me; the idea was impossible. However Mr Rackham hated hunters — and rightly so — he would never have deliberately failed to discharge his father's will correctly.

"I believe," I said, with all the gentility trained into me by my governesses, my school teachers and my sister. "Mr Fairbanks is handsome and charming and told you exactly what you wished to hear. Your disdain for Mr Rackham was easy to mark from a distance; a dashing soldier swooped in to take advantage, spinning a story guaranteed to feed that disdain."

"Some people are only worthy of disdain," said Miss Laura Bellamy.

"I quite agree," I said, and rose to my feet.

A momentary look crossed her face as if she thought I might leave her there; I was rather tempted to let her believe it a little longer. But at that moment. I heard Mr Muggins calling Laura's name from the greenhouse above.

"Down here, sir!" I called, in a fluttery voice. "I'm afraid Miss Laura has sprained her ankle. Thank goodness for a dashing rescuer."

CHAPTER 10

CHAMBREY MAKES A DECISION

The ball did not recover from the re-appearance of Miss Laura Bellamy and her sprained ankle. Mr Muggins and his rescue was hampered somewhat by the sudden spring shower that decided to empty itself from above just as we left the greenhouse. The rescue effort met with further difficulties when it became evident that Laura did not wish either of us to touch her; she suffered the arm of Mr Muggins, in the end, because it was the only way she could make her way back into the ballroom while pretending I did not exist.

The rain had sent all the guests in from the terrace, and had made rather sad work of the paper lanterns and the floral swing.

Somehow I could not bring myself to set foot back into the house. This had nothing to do with the scene within — I could hear perfectly well from where I stood that Mrs Bellamy was on top form, screeching about the harm that had been done to her poor, defenceless daughter — even the quartet stopped playing after a while, presumably so that the guests who remained could more easily witness the entire Bellamy drama.

Were this any other ball, I would have been the first to find a good position so as to see and hear everything that unfolded, and whisper gleefully about it to my friends. But I had no friends here, and I was suddenly so very tired; worn down by living in a place where we were strangers, and everyone else had known each other forever.

It was like the first year of school all over again; rather crushing, if one did not make the best of it. Much like the first year of school, I had not made the best of it in Merry-wist. I could have made friends and charmed them all like Chambrey did, if I'd cared to make the effort. Instead, I had wasted most of my time indulging in an outrageous sulk.

I resolved to stand in the rain until I caught a cold. Why not? It had worked for dear Leda.

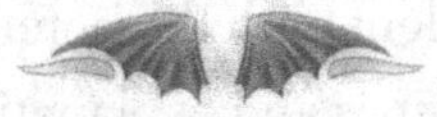

SOMEONE CAME TO FIND ME, eventually. The only surprise was that it was Chambrey.

Any other person coming to find a young lady in the rain might bring her a shawl and encourage her inside; my brother brought the most ridiculously large coat, only suitable for riding, and draped it so thoroughly around my shoulders that I all but disappeared.

"The ball is over," he informed me in grave tones.

"It's all my fault, I suppose."

Chambrey tugged me underneath the small awning, so that at least the cold rain was no longer directly falling on me. The only light streamed through the windows, as the paper lanterns had been extinguished in the wet. "What makes you say that?"

I peeked at him from beneath the enormous collar of the coat. "Darling brother, do not attempt to sweeten the sting."

"I won't pretend," he said after a moment. "That I'm not fascinated to hear the circumstances under which you pushed Miss Laura Bellamy down a flight of stairs."

I let out a squeak of outrage. "Is *that* what she told people?"

"That, dear sister, is the mild version. By the time her mother was bundling her out the front door, the story had grown rather worse."

At moments like these it would be useful to be the sort of young lady who easily burst into tears; a marvellous and enviable talent with the potential to lever one out of all sorts of scrapes and explanations. Sadly for me, my eyes remained dry except for the rainwater that continued to drip from my floral hair arrangement down my eyelashes and directly into my bosom.

"Do *you* think I pushed her down a flight of stairs?" I wondered, out of idle curiosity.

Chambrey nudged me with his elbow and gave me a

grin that was remarkably warm, given the circumstances. My brother has endless wells of forgiveness. "Sweet Dimity," he said. "No one knows better than I that if you wished to push someone down a flight of stairs, you would never be caught in the act."

We were teasing, as we often did, but my laughter got stuck in my throat. I hadn't thought I was worried that he might take the side of the pretty, popular Bellamy family over me, and yet... part of me had in fact feared that outcome. "She was vile about Mr Rackham," I volunteered.

"Yes, I know that too." I stared up at Chambrey; he seemed rather impatient with me. "I know it pleases you and Dido to behave as if I am some innocent baby rabbit with heart-shaped eyes who sees no evil in the world, but I am perfectly capable of noticing when an assembly is lit up by mean-spirited gossip. And on the word of Gideon Fairbanks, of all people!"

Thank goodness. I had not wanted to be the one to explain it all to him. "Is Dido terribly cross?"

"Cross with you? No. Cross with the town of Merry-wist? Oh, yes. I rather think she was about ready to push Miss Laura down the stairs herself by the time they all left."

I let out a breath of relief. I didn't care if the town came after me with pitchforks, as long as my family were on my side. "That will make the rest of our stay rather awkward."

Chambrey took both my hands — which were admit-tedly very cold — and tucked them both inside the pockets of the heavy coat he had inflicted upon me. "That rather depends. What's the date, Dimity?"

"The fourteenth, of course." I had written it in perfect calligraphy on every invitation until it was emblazoned on the inside of my eyelids.

"If we can be ready to leave by lunchtime tomorrow, we can reach Abberline in time for you and Dido to attend the Vigil."

I gaped at him. "Are you certain? Really?"

"Rackham and Dido are already arranging our bags to be packed."

I threw myself at him in a lightning hug. "Thank you," I cried into his ribcage.

"Call it an apology," said Chambrey.

"No, wait." I pulled back. It was exasperating, the way he had kept growing and growing, head and shoulders above me, after we spent most of our childhood being exactly the same size. Such inequity should never be allowed between twins. I hated having to crane to look at him properly. "Why should you apologise? I've been simply dreadful about the whole business."

"You've been miserable," he corrected. "I knew you were miserable. I took you away from the city and pretended your complaining was the usual sort of trivial bumph about other ladies buying the same bonnet, or similar nonsense."

"I will let that pass because you are clearly distraught beyond all reason," I said severely. "Pray, continue your apology."

My brother grinned at me again, that effortless

friendly flashing of teeth that led so many young ladies to believe that Chambrey Iverwold was Prince Charming in a waistcoat. "You look forward to the Season of Dragons every year, and I dragged you to the back of beyond for my own selfishness. I should have made more effort to leave you in town..."

As if that would have worked.

"And I knew you would not," he went on, surprising me for a second time that evening. "It might be a bore that you and Dido are so very protective of me, but I do take advantage, rather. I knew you would not let me be alone."

It was, as it happened, a very good apology. Much more of it and I would become the sort of girl who burst into tears, and no one wanted that on their conscience.

"My ears are cold," I informed him.

Chambrey looked relieved. "We should go inside."

"No, indeed. I wish to hear more about what marvellous sisters we are. Loyal and protective and..." My voice wavered a little, but I managed myself. "Really, Chambrey, you're quite decided?"

"We're going home," he promised me. "No more Elderflower Hall."

CHAPTER 11

MARRYING MR MUGGINS

There was no reason in the world that I should feel bad about Leda, and yet when I woke up the next morning, giddy with the delicious thought that we would return home to the city in only a handful of hours, the very first thing I felt was bad for dear Leda Bellamy.

I was still in two minds as to whether she had any hopes of Chambrey as her future husband, and in no mind at all to encourage her falsely (now that my brother had seen her family's true colours, the notion of marriage between them was twice as impossible as before). Still, Leda had been a guest in our home and, unlike her sister, had not burned our tentative friendship into ash and bone on her way out the door.

She had warned me what her sister was saying, and she had believed Chambrey's character reference for Mr Rackham over the poison dripped in Miss Laura's ear by Gideon Fairbanks. The least she deserved was a letter.

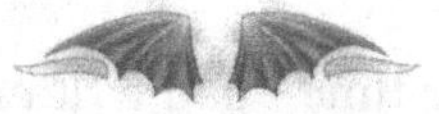

MY DEAR LEDA,

I have arranged for this letter to be handed to you tomorrow, after we have gone. Mr Iverwold, Mr and Mrs Harefield, our dear Mr Rackham and I are all withdrawing to the city for the remainder of the season. I do not expect us ever to return to Merrywist, despite holding the year-lease on Elderflower Hall.

Yours is a quaint and charming town, but I do not pretend to regret leaving it behind.

My sister and I enjoyed our conversations with you and wish you all the best for the future. I do hope we shall continue our acquaintance by correspondence, which shall surely lessen the pain of so sudden a separation.

Your very dear friend,
Dimity Iverwold

THAT SHOULD DO IT. Sickly sweet and mostly insincere, as was the fashion for ladies in correspondence. The sensible thing would be to ask the housekeeper or the butcher's boy to deliver the note; it was hardly worth putting on a stamp when their house was only six fields away (or however distances are measured in these parts).

However, by the time I had written it, I was also feeling slightly bad about Miss Allicot Ellis, with whom I had not even exchanged three words at the ball. Still, she was the only other lady who had sought out my company during our stay. If I hadn't been so determined to keep a moat of distance between me and everyone in this wretched town, we might well have become genuine friends.

I decided to call on Miss Ellis personally, so that no one might say my family had left town without due courtesies. I would then request that she deliver the letter to Miss Bellamy on my behalf. The added benefit of this was that I did not have to be underfoot while Dido ran around Elderflower Hall telling the maids everything they were doing wrong; she is generally kinder to them when there are no witnesses.

Miss Ellis was such a friend to the Bellamys, it would be interesting to know what story she had been told about Miss Laura and the staircase. If she barred her door to me, I would have my answer.

AS IT HAPPENED, the squire's house was experiencing its own upheaval when I arrived, and my having thrown

Laura Bellamy down a staircase was of no interest to anyone.

Miss Allicot Ellis took one look at me, blurted "tea in the garden!" and took the excuse to flee her own drawing room in which her younger sister Sophiar was comforting their weeping mama, while her father poured a distressingly large balloon of porter into himself and grinned maniacally at the wallpaper.

"What on earth has occurred?" I asked as Miss Ellis led me to a darling little outdoor nook with tables and chairs and a singular lack of over-emotional relatives. A maid brought us tea, looking equally glad to be away from the drawing room of doom.

"I am to be married," Miss Ellis said in a low whisper, as if this were a shocking confession. Then she took a deep breath and squared her shoulders, allowing a smile of pride to take over her face. "I am to be married," she said again, with gusto.

"May I wish you every happiness," I said immediately. "Who is the gentleman?" It was news to me that there was anyone eligible in Merrywist outside my own household, and I could be reasonably certain that Miss Ellis had not netted Chambrey or Rackham without my hearing of it.

"Mr Muggins," said Miss Ellis, bracing herself for criticism.

"Oh, I see!" Perhaps the dashing rescue of Miss Laura had made him a more attractive prospect; in truth, the fact that he would someday steal the inheritance of the

Bellamy daughters might be enough to make one overlook both his face and his personality, though I should never say such things out loud. "I thought he wanted Laura?"

Oh, *Dimity*. Speaking of things I should not have said aloud.

"I'm so sorry," I added, far too late. "I did not mean..."

But Miss Ellis was smiling. "You're right, of course," she said with remarkable generosity. "He asked Laura this morning. But she was in such a temper after the ball — her ankle is quite sprained, you know, and... well, she was not as tactful as she might have been."

It was news to me that Laura Bellamy was capable of tact on a good day. "She turned him down?"

"She believed they were ill-suited," said Miss Ellis, demonstrating her own superior grasp of tact.

It was odd to sit here discussing Laura Bellamy as if she had not effectively declared war against me the night before. Why was Merrywist only coming alive with fascinating gossip once I was on my way out of the place?

"As you know, Miss Laura and I do not currently see eye to eye," I said, sipping my cup of tea. "But I agree with her in this. I can't imagine a person less suitable than she to become a curate's wife. Still, it must have been a disappointment to Mr Muggins."

Enough, clearly, to reject his previous plan to offer his hand and house to one of his cousins; one could not blame him, since the younger three sisters were basically children and there was no reason why he had not been allowed to try for Leda in the first place.

"There was quite the scene," Miss Ellis blurted,

somewhat red about the face. "I believe Mrs Bellamy tried to convince Mr Muggins that Laura needed to be asked more than once, and he was so cross at the idea that anyone might play those sort of games, you know, when the lady says no but means yes…"

"I have never in my life met a lady who said no while meaning yes," I informed her. "And I know a great many people."

"In any case, he stormed out, and our house is rather nearby. Mr Muggins marched in here and asked my father for my hand on the spot."

"Goodness!" I had not imagined the little fellow to be quite so assertive. "You must have accepted."

Miss Ellis nodded wildly before I had even asked the question. "I did. I was not too proud at all to say *yes please*. But now Laura's mama is so *angry*, and I am worried Laura will hate me forever."

"I don't see why she should." The whole arrangement was perfectly sensible. Mr Muggins had taken the honourable path in offering his hand to one of the daughters whose inheritance he was to burgle in future years; it was quite unreasonable to expect him to keep harassing the one who said no, when there were more obliging brides available.

"We will inherit her house!" Miss Ellis burst into tears.

Oh, tears. My own failure to master that particular ladylike accomplishment always left me rather at sea when other ladies performed it; thank goodness that

Dido, like I, was no natural weeper or we should not get on nearly as well as we do.

"A terribly long way off," I assured her, pushing the teapot in her direction in the hope that a refreshed cup would cheer her. "If fifteen dragons didn't kill Mr Bellamy, he must be perfectly hardy. Besides, Laura didn't want the fellow." I paused, a little concerned for my new friend. "Do *you* want him? Really?" I tried not to make it sound like I was asking her opinion on boiled sago.

Miss Ellis heaved a sigh, and smiled wanly through her tears. "I'm not romantic. I've never wanted some dreamy lord on horseback to carry me off. I distrust pretty people. All I want is a house and a purpose... and to get away from this town."

That, I could understand. And while Laura Bellamy would make the world's worst curate's wife, it was hard not to see this future Mrs Muggins doing terribly well in the role. "I admire your pragmatism," I assured her. "Before my first season, I was concerned that I would be like my brother, so easily swayed by a friendly face. One amiable dance and I might agree to the most appalling marriage simply because of well-timed smile or a compliment."

Miss Ellis tilted her head at me. "And what happened?"

I shrugged it off. "As it turns out, I cannot find a man entirely handsome unless he shares all of my opinions. It narrows the field drastically but has so far kept me safe from unwise matrimonial choices."

"You *don't* think I'm making an unwise matrimonial choice?" said Miss Ellis, sounding stunned.

"Only you can answer that. Clearly, your parents have their own opinions." From the scene in the drawing room, I was willing to vouchsafe that she had one for the match and one against.

"Papa thought I was on the shelf, I've never seen a man so relieved! But Mama burst into tears at the thought of it, and Sophiar keeps frowning and asking *if I am sure.*"

"If you think marrying Mr Muggins will give you the life you wish, then by all means," I said airily. "Marry Mr Muggins. This is one of the few choices ladies are given over our lives. We owe it to ourselves to chuse a husband that pleases us, not the world."

If more ladies could be *sensible* about marriage like Miss Ellis, I might have not spent the last several months worrying so much about Chambrey's prospects.

"You said Mr Muggins had a patroness," I remembered. "That's good. You'll have someone to consult when you hold dinner parties. Is she a very prestigious dragon? Shall you live near her home?"

"I rather think you'll approve of that part," said Miss Ellis, wiping her eyes. "Mr Muggins has the esteemed patronage of none other than Lady Beautrice de Bramble."

"My dear!" I exclaimed, and gave her a squeezing hug that surprised us both with its effusiveness. "Why didn't you *begin* with that? Of course you must marry him! With Lady de Bramble in your corner, how can you help but be happy?"

As I LEFT the Ellis house, rather pleased with myself for being an excellent helpmeet to Miss Ellis just as she had been abandoned by her other friends, I happened to find the inestimable nephew of Lady Beautrice de Bramble waiting for me in the lane.

"Mr Rackham!" I exclaimed. We had not seen each other since the opening of the ball.

He tipped his hat to me. "Miss Iverwold. May I walk you back?"

"You may."

Country walks with unmarried gentleman aren't exactly recommended for young ladies who seek to preserve their reputations, but it was only Mr Rackham. I tucked my arm into his. "Are you as pleased as I am to be returning to Abberline?"

"I do not regret leaving Merrywist," he said after a moment's contemplation.

"Why, that's exactly what I said in my farewell letter to the elder Miss Bellamy!"

"I'm sure she appreciated the sentiment," he replied dryly. "And somehow you have managed to make Iverwold believe it was his idea to withdraw."

"It was his idea," I said in all honesty.

Mr Rackham gave me an admiring look. "Flawless work. Not that he's all that interested in Miss Bellamy..."

"Indeed, he is not," I confirmed.

"But you and I know how easily that wind might change. Better to get out ahead of the weather."

"My very thought."

It was a little dishonest to let him think my only reason for leaving was to save Chambrey from an inopportune marriage, but I rather liked Rackham thinking me so clever; there would be no benefit in dissuading him of his illusions.

After the showers of yesterday, we were treated to a lovely burst of sunshine as we strolled along the lane. It was enough to make one think that the country was not completely terrible.

"I understand you have been duelling other young ladies for my honour," Mr Rackham remarked.

I scoffed at him. "If only we could! Life would be much simpler if ladies were allowed to duel."

"Yours might be. I imagine mine would become ever more complicated."

I suppose he did have a sister. Mind you, the thought of the sweet and innocent Tatiana Rackham taking up swords was rather amusing. "You do not think your sister would defend your honour in a duel to the death?"

"Apparently she will not need to," he said, and his gaze when it fell on me was almost as warm as the spring sunshine.

It was enough to make a lady feel she was being courted!

"You do know that I didn't *actually* push Laura Bellamy down a staircase," I said, as we turned a corner, and the familiar edifice of Elderflower Hall came into view.

"It's always best to deny such things," he agreed. "I believe her uncle is a solicitor."

I frowned. "It was an accident."

"I believe you entirely."

Did he, though?

"You're teasing me," I grumbled.

Ahead of us, I could see Dido waving her arms as our luggage was loaded into the chaise.

"I would never do such a thing," said Mr Rackham, his eyes dancing. "After all, you're a dangerous lady. You might push me down a staircase..."

CHAPTER 12
THE COUNTESS OF CHAMBREY

There are no words to express how wretched it is to have a patroness who sleeps.

I suppose it's also rather terrible to not have a patron at all, to have never felt that security and comfort... but once one has had a nice thing, being without it must surely warrant a far deeper hollow feeling than never having had it at all.

It was like that with our mother, the sweetest and kindest and... oh, most comfortable of people. I was five when she died, so I barely remember her. The hole in my heart where she lived is perfectly manageable most days. But Dido, who had five more years to know and love her, has a mother-shaped ache behind her ribs that is far deeper than my own.

It helped that I had a twin; it is difficult to miss people when your own particular person is so very close and agreeable, which is how it was with Chambrey and myself until somewhere about the age of twelve when separate schools, and societal nonsense about ladies and gentlemen began to build walls between us. (Despite all that I still had Dido, who did her best to mother me when I needed mothering, though somehow it has never worked in the other direction no matter how hard I try.)

In any case, for the first eight years of my life, we *also* had the most glorious dragon in the country as our family patroness, and then the Countess of Chambrey went to sleep and did not wake up. We did not know we had been abandoned at first, but as every year passed it became a little more evident that this was no mere extended hibernation.

(Chambrey, like our Papa before him, was named after the original lands of our Countess, though the county itself no longer exists; she is three hundred and eighty years old and keeps her title as a courtesy because one does not take things away from dragons if one wishes to remain unscorched.)

The Countess knew everyone. She told tales of my grandmother and mother; every ball they attended, every gown they wore. She held all our secrets. Her scales were the most brilliant emerald green shading all the way to the palest jade on the tips of her wings. Her wyvern body, unhindered by the extraneous limbs of a standard dragon, was long and lithe; she would coil herself up before the fireplace, tucking her two tiny feet beneath the slender muscles of her elongated torso.

(She was coiled now, her body wrapped up like a basket in order to perch her cold grey stone shape upon the wide plinth.)

She was kind to me, in that condescending sort of way that elderly ladies tolerate very small children as long as they mind their manners. I miss her.

In that Season of Dragons, after we returned from Elderflower Hall, I still believed she would return to us. How could she not?

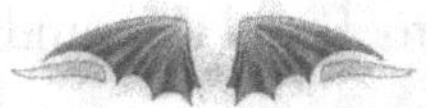

OUR PARTY ARRIVED BACK in the city by torchlight. The driver pulled the chaise-and-four into the muse behind Dido's townhouse, so as to access the stable.

Dido and I hopped out quickly; she had sent her maid Marjoram ahead on the mail cart so that she was here waiting for us, curling irons at the ready.

We primped at record speed, dressing in our best outdoor wear including embroidered mantles and cloaks with hoods. No jewels; we were going to a park, not an assembly room.

Chambrey and Rackham still lingered in the front hall when we emerged. I saw a moment of hesitation in my brother's eyes; normally I would take advantage of such a weakness, but Rackham put a firm hand on his arm and gave me a challenging look.

A deal was a deal, and a lady always knows when to accept gracious defeat.

Mr Harefield appeared in a pressed suit, which was a

miracle unto itself. He escorted Dido and I out into the street in comfortable silence.

We were only three blocks from Hydde Park; it was an easy walk. All the better to fully embrace the pleasure of being back where we belonged.

Coloured lanterns were strung in the streets; occasional winged silhouettes flitted across the moon. We passed the Porteous Museum, to see sizzling salamanders crawling all over its roof, and the candlelight of a reception flickering inside.

I refused hot chestnuts at the gates of the park; I have not enjoyed them since over-indulging a few years ago. Still, Mr Harefield bought us cups of cider and I was not so churlish as to turn that down, nor the frangipane tart he broke into three even pieces for us to share. It was not a warm evening, and my gloves were thin.

Here, finally, the glories of the Season unfurled before us. Crowds milled around the park, entertained by flame dancers and a brass band. We stopped to purchase candles at one stall, incense at another, and a wreath of fresh apple blossom at a third.

We strolled along the Serpentyne, watching the young dragons at play in the water. There are several rivers and sacred lakes dotted across the parks of the city, but this one has always been a favourite of dragon-kind.

There were statues everywhere: the forms of sleeping dragons. Empty plinths, as well, waiting for winter when the dragons will lay themselves down in the most comfortable places they can.

Not every dragon may sleep in Hydde Park. In the

old days, one had to belong to a High Family, or a line of ancient glory. More and more, only the very oldest and youngest of dragon-kind are drawn to this place.

The oldest and most respected of dragons have exclusive plinths, carved with sigils warning that the space is reserved in perpetuity. No random bluescale or greyling kit may climb aboard for an afternoon's snooze.

Mr Harefield led the way into the Birch Avenue, carrying a hired lantern he had acquired on the street. Dido and I walked behind, arm in arm. Here, among the trees, in amongst the empty plinths, several bodies of sleeping dragons remained captured in eternal stone. Most had families present, at least one or two diligent representatives, and sometimes whole sprawling parties.

We passed the Nelwethers, a mob of cousins and aunties busily scrubbing moss off the plinth belonging to the Honourable Charleuse Cottering, who had been asleep longer than I had been alive. They had brought a picnic and were chattering happily amongst themselves as if it was a birthday celebration and not a vigil.

We passed Lord Peregrine Annesley, a small and bushy-eyebrowed gentleman dragon who once exchanged pleasantries with me at my coming out ball. His client humans, the Terminster-Bollivar families, looked rather thin-lipped and distressed; perhaps this was the first spring that their dragon had remained in hibernation.

I caught the eye of Bessie Terminster, who was wearing an extremely pretty new dress, and a charming bonnet in the new fashion. She gave me a little wave and a smile.

So, it seemed I had not been entirely socially destroyed by my disappearance for half of the Season; this was intelligence of vital import.

I RATHER LIKED that the Countess of Chambrey's plinth, complete with its more recent Iverwold family carvings, was so deep into the Birch Avenue. This meant there would have been fewer witnesses to notice if we had left our dragon unattended on the most important night of the year; now that we were present after all, it was rather nice to place the candles, light the incense and arrange the wreath without spying eyes to judge us.

We were far enough from the festive end of the park that the echoing trumps of the brass band were muted, echoing gently through the trees.

We spoke the words and performed the rituals.

We waited, kneeling on the grass until the damp soaked into our skin.

IT IS SAID that the Vigil is an entreaty, a wake-up call and a final reminder all rolled together. For those dragons locked deep in their chilly slumber, when they hear the soft prayers of their people and smell our gifts, they know that they are loved — many of them drift further into their hibernation to shut out all distractions for the year. But some...

Some dragons hear the prayers for the invitation that they are. There are always a few stragglers who do not wake until the Vigil, enjoying the warm attention when their skin bleeds back into bright colour, and they slide their claws off the slippery marble plinths.

For some families, the Vigil is a night of celebration.

For others, it is a quiet acknowledgment that dragons do not owe us their company; if they wish to keep sleeping, they will do exactly that.

Dido and Mr Harefield and I waited until midnight; the Countess did not stir.

Finally, when we arose cold and aching from the ground and made our way back through the avenue of trees, we came upon the red-faced, merry party of the Nelwether family, beside themselves with joy that the Honourable Charleuse Cottering's left front foot was now a vivid shade of rose-pink, the claws on her right front foot were gleaming gold, and look, her eyes were cracking open...

We congratulated them with all the enthusiasm we

could muster — it was indeed one for the history books —
and then we went home.

I GAVE up on sleep sometime after three o'clock and went
downstairs to the parlour. Dido's townhouse does not
feature a library, but the parlour is the warmest room in
the middle of the night, as it takes forever for the fire in
the iron grate to die down completely.

I found, to my entire lack of surprise, the lamps still
blazing and my brandy-soused brother laid out on a
couch that was exactly 3/4 of his length.

"Nice night?" I inquired.

Chambrey made a low humming sound that
suggested either that he was terribly relaxed or on the
verge of tomorrow's headache hitting him early. "You?"

"Uneventful," I informed him, sitting primly on the
couch opposite.

Chambrey cracked an eye open. "Sorry," he
muttered.

I shrugged. It was not as if I had expected a miracle.
"It helped to be there." I paused, summoning up my
entire personal supply of empathy. "Did it help you to…
not be there?"

"Yes," he said fervently.

"Well, then. That's all right." To my surprise, it was.
It had been refreshing to take comfort in Dido and Mr

Harefield's wordless presence, embracing my own feelings of abandonment and melancholy without having to constantly check on Chambrey's countenance in order to gauge his state of mind.

By the looks of it, he had likewise spent the evening avoiding his own state of mind. Nothing wrong with that on occasion; he had been with Mr Rackham, after all. It was not as if they could have tripped into too much trouble.

The blackened coals on the fire cracked and spluttered. Exhausted, I sank back into the couch. I should go to bed, but it was rather comfortable to pause here for a moment, watching over my brother.

Chambrey sighed, rolled on to his back in a contortion that could not possibly be comfortable (parlour furniture is not designed for gentlemen's spines) and began to talk. "Do you remember the Vigil after Father's funeral?"

Oh, that was a wretched time. We were sent home from school for two weeks of mourning. As a fourteen-year-old who had barely been allowed a glimpse of the Season at that point, I was caught between the guilty pleasure of dragon spotting and the overwhelming weight of Papa being gone.

Dido had the worst of it, barely home from her honeymoon Grand Tour, and now obliged to manage everything from selecting our oldest silk pelisses to dye black, to hosting a funeral tea for two hundred at the busiest time of the year when there were no extra kitchen staff to be hired.

I spent days sewing black crepe to bonnets, glad to be

doing *something*, and resenting that Chambrey need to do nothing but wear an armband on his usual suit.

Mr Rackham came to stay, which was helpful, and then Lady Beautrice de Bramble turned up to occupy Dido's best guest room, which was quite the opposite of helpful. Bad enough that we were children trying to perform funeral rites to society standards, but now we were not even safe from disapproval in our own home...

My home, I had realised, at the time. I would not be returning to Papa's latest rented townhouse. We had to remove all our things, as the lease was due before the summer holidays. Chambrey and I would be living with Dido now, when not in school.

It was all so much. I remembered getting furious at Chambrey because he had gone all grim and quiet, and was never around when I wanted to howl into a cushion.

Now, with the lamps low and the remains of a fire crackling in Dido's best parlour, I looked across at my grownup brother on the couch and wondered for the first time what he had been thinking, during those terrible two weeks.

"The Vigil was three days after the funeral," I murmured. I had felt sick from eating too many roasted chestnuts, and so self-conscious as we did our rituals without Papa for the first time. Dido dragged us home early, claiming the weather was about to turn bad and she did not want us to get colds...

"I went back," Chambrey confessed. "Snuck out of the house in the middle of the night and went off to Hydde Park on my own."

"And Dido didn't skin you alive?" I wondered.

"She waited two hours, then sent Rackham after me."

"Of course she did." Even at a mere nineteen years old, Dido had been far too knowing for her own good.

"I knelt at the Countess's feet for what felt like forever," Chambrey confessed in a whisper. "It didn't seem possible to me that she would abandon us. She had only been gone six years or so at that point — plenty of dragons sleep longer and still come back."

It was fourteen years now, and I had not relinquished all hope.

"Everyone kept saying I was the man of the house," Chambrey said bitterly. "All those strangers at the funeral. Papa's friends. I felt the weight of it — of looking after Dido and you, though you're both much cleverer than I am. We didn't even have a family home. And I thought, surely... she'll *know*. The Countess won't make us do this without a dragon."

Oh, my poor darling. "Did Rackham drag you home by the scruff of your collar?"

Chambrey shook his head. "He kept me company until dawn, then took me out to breakfast at a chophouse. We talked. He'd always been — you know, rather aloof with us before that."

"We were brats," I remembered fondly, thinking of all those summers playing pranks on Rackham, teasing him.

"That night, he spoke like we were friends, equals. He told me he felt just as hollow as me when his father died — he still had his mother, but she was sickly and

could not help much. And he *had* Lady Beautrice."
Chambrey shivered.

I rose without thinking and found one of the knitted blankets that Dido likes to make in the brief intervals between her friends having babies. I draped it over my brother, and then returned to the couch opposite.

"One thing I remember most clearly," mumbled Chambrey. "Rackham told me having a dragon patroness alive and well and looking out for one's interests wasn't entirely... well. It didn't make the weight any lighter. If anything, it added another responsibility to your shoulders."

"And that helped?"

"So much," said Chambrey with heat.

We remained in comfortable silence after that, for quite a while. It was strange how two people could grow up together, exactly the same age, and still have such different histories.

"Dimity," Chambrey said with a yawn, as the last coals of the fire crumbled to nothing. "Is there anything you want to tell me about Mr Rackham?"

I didn't have the faintest idea what he might be angling for, unless it was an update on the Laura Bellamy situation, about which the least said the better. "I'm not going to let him marry anyone unsuitable, if that's what you mean."

"No," said Chambrey, looking amused. "I don't imagine you will."

CHAPTER 13
TAKING TEA IN A FASHIONABLE STREET

After the vigil, only six weeks remained of this year's Season of Dragons. Another young lady might sulk about what she had missed, but I was determined to make the most of the time I had left.

It. Was. Marvellous.

In the first week, I invited Kitty and Emma over to take tea. Together, we combed through the invitations and calling cards that had banked up while I was away. I sighed and groaned my regrets through all of the lost opportunities and missed once-in-a-lifetime social events, and then I let them go.

There would always be more parties.

I attended a sunset picnic hosted by the Misses Benedictine in the gardens of the Winter Palace. I joined Dido in supporting the Royal Fundraising Bazaar for wingless kits.

By the end of that first week, it felt as if I had never been away.

Mr Rackham departed for Malachite, where he was to spend a few weeks with his sister Tatiana before returning to us for the final fort-night of the season, but Chambrey was perfectly amiable even without his friend at his side, and often went to his club to socialise with other companions. I was relieved to observe that his countenance showed no glimpse of melancholy about our hasty departure from the country.

As for me — I was the very *opposite* of melancholy.

IN THE SECOND WEEK, our household were invited to a celebration breakfast at Nelwether Grange, welcoming home the family's newly awoken dragon, the Honourable Charleuse Cottering. I was honoured to exchange polite conversation with our noble hostess, and even took home a piece of marzipan sponge decorated with a single perfect claw mark.

IN THE THIRD WEEK, I attended the Black and White Ball at the Coterie, the most exclusive of all assembly rooms in Abberline, an event hosted by the esteemed wyvern Mrs Walpole who had, against all the odds, extended invitations to Chambrey and myself, despite us having neglected her previous courtesies in our absence from the city. I danced under the stars with eight eligible gentlemen, and was called upon the next morning by four of them. Dido's cook quite ran out of currant scones and seed cake!

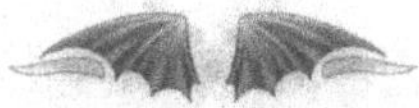

IN THE FOURTH WEEK, after an unforgettable exhibition of dragonfire at the Pleasure Gardens, I received a proposal of marriage from a Bellazian Baron, who did not suit me in the least but accepted my rejection in remarkable good spirits.

IN THE FIFTH WEEK, Dido refused to speak to me for several days because of turning down the Bellazian Baron. She only forgave me after I agreed to attend her book club with the terrifying Lady Beautrice de Bramble, who had surprised us (and our recently-returned Mr Rackham most of all) by arriving suddenly in the city.

One thing you can say about Lady de Bramble, she loves to keep her nephew on his toes.

In the sixth and final week, Dido and I took tea with Miss Leda Bellamy.

Of all the fashionable tea shops in all the fashionable streets of Abberline, one cannot do better than Melleins. Chatsworth Cakes has the daintiest petits four, and Deboling & Daughters is the favourite of the Princess Royal, but there is something about the sheer undiluted elegance of Melleins, with its lemon and rose striped awning and perfect porcelain teacups that makes one feel as if one *is* the Princess Royal.

Best of all: it is favoured by the most fashionable dragons.

There are only two window tables, set on enormous, raised platforms with plenty of stretching space for wings and tails. The East Window can house up to three dragons and another three human guests, depending on length and wingspan.

Today, the lavender-violet scales of Great Aunt Edith Highwater were on display, this enormous aunt comfortably spread across 5/6ths of the polished boards, while my school acquaintance Myfanwy and several of her female relatives clustered on dainty chairs on the other side of the tea table. When Great Aunt Edith paused in lecturing them to open her mighty maw, the youngest of the cousins (I believe her name was Mary-Ann) would lever several buttered muffins on to her Great Aunt's tongue by means of an antique toasting fork.

There were other dragons here, gathered on the mezzanine floor and basking in the sunlight from several high windows. The mezzanine was for the exclusive use of dragons, as many preferred to drink tea and eat cakes without bothering about dainty saucers, or human manners.

Miss Bellamy looked desperately uncomfortable, perching on a chair in the centre of the tea shop in her best muslin, twitching each time she heard a growl or a swish.

I wondered for one uncharitable moment whether Dido had guessed this would be our guest's reaction to Melleins and had selected the venue accordingly.

We had not expected the letter announcing Miss Bellamy's arrival in Abberline, barely a month after our own departure. I had written, of course, to perform the kind of compulsory platitudes that were drilled into ladies in the schoolroom: how to be polite in perfect handwriting while keeping one's acquaintances at a safe distance.

Leda had written back a similar missive of no importance, and it seemed we would leave it there — no ill will between us, but no particular intimacy going forth.

But then she wrote again. This time it was to announce that she was coming to Abberline to stay with relatives on the outskirts (a Mr & Mrs Gracechurch of Gardiner Street) and would be charmed if the ladies of our household had a spare afternoon on which to receive her.

I had convinced myself that our concerns about Chambrey being in danger of an unwise match were largely shaped by the mama's intentions and not those of the young lady, who was blameless in her family's machinations. Was I wrong?

Dido who had been so measured in her handling of the Bellamys in their own territory, leaped into defensive mode. "Miss Bellamy and Chambrey must not see each other," she decided over her breakfast tray (I had brought in the mail to her immediately on seeing the return address). "Their over-familiar behaviour in Merrywist can be easily passed off as country informality, but if she has followed him here, he may be at genuine risk."

"He does not know about the letter," I informed her. Rackham and Chambrey had headed out early to ride in the park together with some fellows from their club, before the morning post.

"Good," said Dido, biting into her toast in a vengeful manner. "Let it be ladies only. We'll send the little fortune hunter packing."

I had begun to think myself that it might not be the end of the world if Chambrey married Leda; except of course that we would be tied forever to the blood-stained papa, the dreadful mama, and the four sisters who had made an enemy of Mr Rackham (one of whom, it must be said, was well on the way to earning her place as my personal nemesis).

No, of course. Dido was always right. Now that my elder sister had taken command of the situation, I could not but feel relieved. Chambrey's fate was out of my hands.

WE SAT AT MELLEINS, and ate exquisite petits four, and sipped tea, and were perfectly polite to Miss Bellamy (demoted from 'dear Leda' to a more formal mode of address upon her incursion into our city) while she squirmed under the jewelled gaze and haughty disinterest of several of the city's most respectable dragons. She never knew what hit her.

We spoke of the following matters:

- The health of Mr and Mrs Gracechurch, the uncle and aunt with whom Miss Bellamy was pleased to reside during her brief foray to the city. (Excellent, after a visit to Merrywist to improve their lungs.)
- The health of Mr Harefield. (Tolerable, as ever.)
- The health of Miss Bellamy's sisters, her mother and father. (Quite well, thank you,

with no specific reference to sprained ankles or broken legs.)
- The health of Mr Chambrey Iverwold and his friend Mr Rackham. (Much improved for their return to the city, with a diverting anecdote about the demands of Mr Rackham's aunt, Lady de Bramble.)
- The wonders of the Season, with particular reference to the Winter Palace picnic and the Black and White ball, but no mention at all of the Bellazian Baron.
- A book that Dido had recently read (and I had not) for the book club so recently graced by the presence of the aforementioned Lady Beautrice de Bramble.
- The upcoming nuptials of Miss Allicot Ellis to the Rev. Mr Muggins of Lower Templeton in Wutheringshire, four weeks hence.

Here at least, my conversation with Miss Bellamy slipped into the territory of interest and enthusiastic chatter; this moment coincided with Dido briefly leaving our table in order to exchange polite greetings with the Highwaters.

During our brief window of informality, I drew from Miss Bellamy that her mama had by no means forgiven Mr Muggins for the perceived slight upon her family in chusing his new bride. Mrs Bellamy had quite forbidden all five daughters from attending the wedding, though they had been expressly invited.

I was in the fortunate position of being able to inform Miss Bellamy that Mr Muggins had extended an invitation to Mr Rackham and his sister, perhaps out of deference to his patron, Lady de Bramble. Miss Ellis had likewise sent our household an invitation; I had not thought to accept until this moment, upon learning that Miss Ellis' oldest friends were banned from the occasion.

"I wish you would," said Miss Bellamy, her eyes shining with kindness. "Allicot deserves all the kindness and support."

I sipped my tea. "We shall see. I do not imagine your sister Miss Laura would approve of my going; nor would she or your mama approve of you taking tea with me."

"Perhaps not," said our guest, looking pained. "And yet I am sure that the troubles between you are naught but a misunderstanding. I could not imagine you capable of anything truly bad."

Dido returned to the table, a little windblown after Great Aunt Edith had huffed steam in her face in a friendly manner. Miss Bellamy blushed and retreated back into herself.

"We were discussing the upcoming wedding of Miss Ellis and Mr Muggins," I informed my sister.

"Indeed," said Dido, tidying her curls. "Do we require more cakes?"

Miss Bellamy was staring at Dido, caught somewhere between awe and fear. "How can you allow yourself so near their mouths?" she whispered. "I would have fainted dead away."

Dido and I stared at her. Around us, the clinking of

teacups and cake forks continued, though the air became a little frostier than before; dragons have excellent hearing.

"To dine in the presence of dragons is an honour and a privilege," said Dido in chilly tones. "I'm sorry your mother left such an important detail out of your education."

There was no recovering the tea party after that; we finished our refreshments and left Melleins under a cloud of awkward silence.

In the street, as we waited for a carriage to take us home, Miss Bellamy was valiant enough to make one more attempt at inquiring after our brother, this time to ask whether he was very busy since his return to the city.

"Terribly busy," said Dido, without making eye contact. "He and Mr Rackham have so many friends, and there are a great many pursuits available to gentlemen in the city."

I opened my mouth to suggest (as I might with any school friend I had tripped over) that Miss Bellamy join me at one of the remaining events of the Season, but one could not take a lady this timid to see serpent racing in the Serpentyne, or the Goldenscales Exhibition in Ganymede Square. She had barely been able to cope with tea at Melleins.

I closed my mouth.

"And of course," said Dido, whipping around to give Miss Bellamy a warm but artificial smile. "We do so hope that soon there will be reason to wish my brother joy in his future happiness, once we are free to announce an engagement."

Miss Bellamy and I stared at her in mutual shock.

"An engagement?" I parroted.

Dido's smile widened, like a crocodile. "We are all so very fond of Mr Rackham's sweet sister Tatiana," she crooned, a phrase that was both true and entirely misleading. "Ah, a carriage. You take this one, Miss Bellamy. Your lodgings are quite in the opposite direction of ours."

With the social graces of a royal footman, she swept Miss Bellamy into the carriage, paid the driver two crowns, and watched them rattle off into the distance. Towards Gardiner Street, I supposed, though I had no idea where that might be.

"Are you serious?" I spluttered. "You think Chambrey and Tatiana...?"

Dido sighed. "Probably not," she admitted. "He's going to need a *very* sensible wife, and sense is not something even a dozen governesses can impose. Give it another five years, though, and she may come up to scratch."

I shook my head at her, not sure whether to be impressed or disapproving. "I rather thought in Merrywist that you were losing your edge."

Dido smiled sweetly at me. "That was the country, and this is Abberline. I may not have wings and flame, but I can still protect my family with as many sharp edges as prove necessary."

THE LAST FEW days of the Season of Dragons came and went, and we did not hear a word more from Miss Bellamy. I can only assume that she returned home to her family. I wished her well, with all my heart.

But I was entirely content to never see a member of the Bellamy family again.

CHAPTER 14

CARNELIANS

There is nowhere in the world as splendid as the Malachite estate, bonded to the Rackham family unto twenty generations. There is certainly nowhere in the world of which I have such fond and enduring memories (leaving aside the matter of Gideon Fairbanks pushing me into a river).

And yet, there is one other manor which fills me with similar levels of awe and longing and childhood nostalgia, though I have only visited but half a dozen times in my life. It is, of course, the magnificent Carnelians Park.

There are houses for old hoarding families, featuring all manner of comforts designed expressly for the convenience of dragons who might visit or even live with said family for some parts of the year.

Then there are houses built for dragons, another matter entirely.

Humans have lived at Carnelians over the years; there is usually a Rackham or two in residence, such as our Mr Rackham's cousin Colonel Fordyce, who stays there when on leave from the army. But make no mistake: Carnelians is a dragon residence, first and foremost. Lady Beautrice de Bramble might be aunt and patron to the Rackham family, but it is she and no other who is lady of this manor.

Carnelians is a handsome modern building, less than two hundred years old, and built directly over the natural entrance to Wutheringshire's extensive underground cave system. Lady Beautrice herself had her home built, gleaming crimson brick by gleaming crimson brick, over the secure hiding place of her hoard.

As is customary for dragon residences, everything about Carnelians is bright and shallow. The steps are deeply cut to allow for large bodies and slithering tails. The doorways are cut in the round to allow Lady B's wings to pass without the indignity of tucking them back against her spine. The many ornamental pathways in the extensive gardens are spacious enough to allow two dragons to walk along them, side by side.

Not everything is practical; like many ladies of advancing years, Lady B has a penchant for antique ornaments and scraps of lace, which does rather make drawing room gatherings something of a challenge: Lady B herself will never admit that her careless wing-flaps or tail-swishes have knocked the porcelain shepherdesses off the piano, or the beaded antimacassars off the side table, and so it is the duty of all humans to catch and reposition such items before she notices anything is amiss.

Still, an invitation to this jewel of houses is a rare

treat, and all the more so when my inclusion is expressly for the entertainment of Lady Beautrice de Bramble's true favourites: her dragon daughter Quartz, and her human niece-by-patronage, Miss Tatiana Rackham.

IT WAS four weeks into summer. Our most recent beautiful (if truncated) Season of Dragons was over, and the time for house parties had properly arrived.

The Rackhams had arrived at Carnelians Park a day ahead of us. I spotted Tatiana and Quartz romping in the garden as our chaise-and-four (containing myself, Chambrey, Dido and Marjoram, with Mr Harefield riding silently on the box with the driver) drew up before the house.

"Rackham will have to let that girl grow up eventually," said Dido with a huff, perhaps recalling that she was not allowed to run about freely when she was ten-and-six.

"Would we not all prefer to return to the careless days of childhood now and then?" said Chambrey with a merry grin, waving to Tatiana as he leaped out of the chaise.

Quartz reached us first, a bounding figure of silver-grey scales and blood-ruby eyes. She was normally to be found sitting wanly at her mother's feet, and so it was lovely to see her enjoying the sunshine with a friend.

"Dimity!" shrieked Tatiana, overtaking Quartz so

quickly that she almost tripped over her tail. "Look, look, isn't it marvellous?" With a casual familiarity, she lifted Quartz's wing to display several glowing rose-pink scales.

"Oh," I said, clapping my hands. "Your colour!"

A dragon's colour coming in is the first sign that she is moving from adolescence to adulthood. Soon Quartz would be thinking about chusing a human — or, more commonly, a married couple — so as to form her first household and build a hoard together. I had no doubt that Lady Beautrice had made her own plans for this eventuality; she was hardly the sort to be caught unawares by such an important development.

"I'm so glad you are here," said Tatiana, curtseying to us as we alighted from the chaise-and-four. If we had been alone, or only ladies were present, I might have expected one of her exuberant hugs, but she had a wary eye on Dido — clearly the latest wave of governesses had taught her to spot a disapproving matron at close quarters. "We are to have lawn games, and my brother said I may attend the wedding!"

That last was no surprise to me. It would have been the height of cruelty for Mr Rackham to bring his sister across the county and bid her stay at home for such a respectable local event. Nevertheless, I made all of the appropriate noises.

LATER, as the maids unpacked the bags into our various rooms — I was honoured with the Tournament Room, featuring a four-poster bed, chivalric tapestries and several ornamental swords hung over grey mock-stone walls — Tatiana slipped in to keep me company while I changed my dress.

"Quartz does not think Aunt Beautrice will want her to do the Season quite as soon as next year," she confided in me. "But I think that best, because my brother insists *I* wait until eighteen to come Out which is a whole year after that. If her colour comes in at this rate, Quartz and I may be able to come to the city for my first Season and we shall be Out together! It will be such fun to have a friend to promenade with."

The Season after next... Miss Rackham with her substantial dowry, going about with a youngling dragon as her best friend. The eligible gentlemen of the Nine Hundred would not know what hit them.

"I will be your friend," I reminded her. "I promised to take you to all the best assemblies!"

"You," huffed Tatiana. "You will be an old married lady by then, staring down your nose at me from afar like Mrs Harefield does."

One had to admire such confidence in the young.

"Unless you know something I do not," I said, glancing at my hair in the mirror to check it was tidy and I needn't bother Marjoram with fixing it before tea. "I shall have to be very quick to catch myself a husband before you come Out and turn all the heads."

Tatiana giggled obligingly at me. "I'm sure there are gentlemen enough for us both, Dimity!"

Such confidence.

THERE WAS TRULY no dragon in the world, alive or sleeping, as formidable as Lady Beautrice de Bramble. If I was told that she was personally responsible for turning half the dragons of the land into stone, I should well believe it.

The lady's scales varied from a bright ruby red to a deep mulberry, with shining wing-points and golden claws. Her eyes were gold as well, and generally full of scorn.

Carnelians was a house of pure formality; ladies and gentlemen behaved in a regimented manner as set out by Lady Beautrice's own aunt, the long-deceased carnelian dragon Lady Corneliar de Bramble, whose portrait hung in every room of the house. (The portrait in my room depicted Lady Corneliar as the mythical Queen Gwenhyfar of the Jade, mere moments before she blasted the lovelorn Prince Percival into ash and bone for his impertinence in accidentally brushing her wing.)

Tea was a gathering for ladies, which occurred between the hours of three and four. Supper included gentlemen, but ladies were dismissed before the cheese and brandy. Any games or amusements were scheduled at least three days in advance.

Today at tea, we were joined in the parlour by Miss Ellis, the bride to be, along with her mother Lady Tylvia and sisters Sophiar and Frunces. It was most common for a bride to be married from her family home before travelling to live with her husband, but of course Lady B would not be inconvenienced by such a tradition.

"I told Mr Muggins," she now declaimed, her voice vibrating every porcelain cup. "Bad enough that he deprived our village of a parson for four weeks in order to find a bride, let alone that he might drag us across the countryside to locate a nothing of a village in the middle of [Something]—shire."

I agreed with the great lady in the matter of Merrywist, but saw Miss Ellis wince at the slight, and felt quite sorry for her.

"Are you looking forward to establishing your own little home?" I asked as scones were loaded before us on the tiniest of tea tables, with such a bounty of jam and cream as I have never seen on any city table.

"Oh, yes," said Miss Ellis, her eyes brightening. "The parsonage is a splendid house, surrounded by a laurel hedge..."

"Mind you don't change a stick of that furniture!" bellowed Lady Beautrice on the far side of the room. "All personally selected by myself and supplied from the attics here in Carnelians, except for the fresh-ticked mattresses which I ordered from Gaummidges on my personal account."

"And of course," said Miss Ellis, with the tight smile of a young lady determined to find the humour in her situation. "Our comfortable home is situated against Carnelians Park with only the green pales between us. It takes a short and most pleasant walk to reach the house, which will allow my husband and myself to visit Lady Beautrice as often as she pleases."

"You shall dine with me twice a week," thundered the dragon, lifting her maw from the enormous silver tea tray on which her own refreshments were laid out for convenient gnawing. "Or I shall wonder why, Miss Ellis."

"The honour would be entirely mine, Lady Beautrice," said Miss Ellis, sweeping into a most deferential curtsey.

THE WEDDING of Miss Ellis and Mr Muggins was exactly as modest and perfect as one might expect of a country parson whose living was trapped under the claw of Lady Beautrice de Bramble.

There were fresh flowers in the church, and we were honoured to gather in the church hall afterwards for tea and sandwiches, if not a full wedding breakfast.

The groom was puffed up and pleased with himself, even if he did spend far more time introducing his guests to his patroness than to his bride; the new Mrs Muggins looked perfectly content with her situation, and her mother managed not to weep in church for which we were all rather grateful.

Lady B attended the wedding, but did not stay for cake. She dragged a mournful Quartz behind her as she poured them both into their enormous barouche with gilded windows.

Mr Rackham did allow Tatiana to stay for cake, and she spent the entire reception demonstrating to him how she had been taught every courtesy that one might require of a young lady shortly to be allowed into proper society.

In any case, Tatiana made fast friends with Miss Ellis' younger sisters. It was nice to catch a glimpse of what it would be like when she was finally unleashed upon the public.

"Next season, perhaps?" I teased Mr Rackham as I caught him observing his sister laughing with her new friends over cucumber sandwiches.

He gave me a stern look. "Did you suffer unduly for waiting until the age of eighteen to attend balls, Miss Iverwold?"

"Not in the least," I said, unfurling my fan. "But thanks to attending school, I had friends to keep me company while I waited."

He made a low grumbling sound, which I usually interpret to mean he has heard, and agrees with me.

"Miss Iverwold," boomed a voice behind me.

The wedding was long over. I had taken the opportunity for a gentle stroll in the park of Carnelians. My solitude was not to be! I had already shared a chance conversation with Colonel Fordyce, who appeared quite determined to charm me over the course of my stay, while making discreetly certain that I was aware he was not available for marriage.

Our conversations generally turned to the one thing we had in common, and so this afternoon (as before) we spent a pleasant half hour exchanging tales of the virtues of his cousin Mr Rackham.

Once he had shuffled away, I hoped to enjoy a little solitude. Alas, I was only halfway along the rose promenade when I was hailed by my hostess.

I turned to see Lady Beautrice striding through a thorny archway, sending bursts of petals into the air with little heed for the plants. I curtseyed, of course.

Gilded in the late afternoon sunlight, the dragon glowed blood-red. She pulled up only a few feet from where I stood, her claws scraping on the soft pebbled surface of the path.

"Lady Beautrice," I greeted her as I rose from my curtsey.

She snorted, and rings of smoke came out of her enormous nostrils. "I understand you are to be credited with my nephew allowing my niece to stay a few weeks longer this summer than originally planned," she said in ringing tones.

I had to think fast; it seemed that Rackham had taken my plea to let Tatiana make friends as encouragement to give her more time with Quartz.

"I am sure your nephew needs no encouragement to spend more time with his family," I said sweetly, in a moment of pure diplomatic genius.

"Indeed, he does not," growled Lady B. She looked me up and down, as if determined to find fault with me. "How old are you, Miss Iverwold?"

"My twin brother and I turn two-and-twenty next month."

"That is far too young for your brother to marry."

"I agree entirely."

"You, though. Should you not have secured a husband by now?"

I thought of the Bellazian Baron who had been handsome, rich and charming. A little too nice for his own good; I would have been bound to make him unhappy. And, of course, he was twenty years my senior. "I have had offers, my lady," I said discreetly.

"Ha! Picky, are you?"

"Exceedingly." Dido certainly thought so.

Lady Beautrice took another step forward; her hot breath engulfed me. Hopefully I would be able to stand the honour without swooning. "My nephew Rackham recently turned eight-and-twenty. He should begin thinking about marriage," she declared. "You and that brother of yours spend more time in his company than I. Did any suitable young ladies catch his eye this Season?"

I blinked, thinking of Miss Laura Bellamy and her fine eyes. *Not exactly suitable, no.* "I believe that Mr Rackham is more concerned about settling Miss Rackham's future before he considers his own," I ventured. There, that should buy him a year or two's grace.

"True enough," Lady B snorted. "The man is all responsibility."

"His devotion to his sister's best interests is entirely creditable."

"Did I say it was not?" She huffed again. I felt the muslin of my day dress wilt under her steam. "I have always intended that when Quartz is of an age to form her household, she should pair-bond with my nephew's future wife," she announced.

Keeping it all in the family, of course. I was not entirely surprised though it was alarming that Lady Beautrice was being so candid with me; perhaps she intended to eat me afterwards so that I could not divulge her secrets.

"That would be an honour indeed," I said. "For the Rackham family to have two such gracious patronesses."

It would be a mild sort of scandal, to be sure... but less so than if Quartz pair-bonded with Rackham himself while he already enjoyed her mother's patronage. Dragons were a bounty that were expected to be spread amongst the Nine Hundred. Bringing them back again through marriage was the only way to collect a set without seeming greedy.

Then again, this was Lady Beautrice de Bramble. Any hint of a scandal would be doused by one scornful look. Should she ever deign to take her rightful place among the Coterie, the matrons there would likely all bow to her, though she had taken little interest in city politics over the years. Carnelians was her kingdom.

"I am not getting any younger," she boomed at me now. "Over three hundred years old. What would happen to my family, should I begin to sleep more heavily in the winters?"

My eyes pricked a little with what could not be tears; for all her fearsome nature, it was lovely to know there was at least one dragon in the world who made preparations for such an occurrence.

"How is the Countess?" Lady Beautrice asked me now, her golden eyes holding me fast, like a magic spell rooting my feet to the ground.

"She sleeps peacefully," I said, my voice trembling only a little under her piercing gaze.

"Yes," growled Mr Rackham's aunt. "That is what I thought."

CHAPTER 15
HOME IS WHERE THE HOARD IS

There is something entirely wretched about being in the city when everyone else has gone to the country for the summer; thanks to the Rackhams extending their stay at Carnelians, our usual trip to Malachite had been postponed.

It felt as if our earlier adventures in Merrywist had turned the whole year upside down, leaving us out of synchronisation with the rest of society; Dido and I were quite determined, however, that Chambrey should not get bored enough to return to Elderflower Hall.

Every time he looked even the slightest bit wistful, one of us must suggest a new entertainment. It had become rather a game of ours, and in the month that followed the Muggins wedding we played quoits in the park, attended the dragon races three times, and spent two weeks at a spa hotel on the coast. This latter adventure was the most successful by far: Chambrey almost fell in love with a splendid bluestocking, but she threw him over so as to continue her research into hermit crab habitats without interruption.

Meanwhile, far more interesting developments were happening elsewhere.

My dear Dimity

You will be delighted to hear that our stay at Carnelians is drawing to a close; it has been all rather lovely but my brother is wearing at the edges after so long in polite proximity to our aunt. We will be travelling home next week, and Ford has promised to open the house up properly to guests before Midsummer.

To our surprise, Aunt Beautrice has given her permission for Quartz to visit with us for the rest of the summer; she will be restricted to only those social occasions that my brother would allow me to attend (which is to say, hardly any) but it will be such fun to have her at my side and I do hope that you and Mr Iverwold and Mrs Harefield (and Mr Harefield if he can stand the joy of it) will join us all on the 14th of the month.

We are all excitement here, for Mrs Muggins has a friend from home visiting — we have not yet heard the name of her visitor, but she is sure to come to tea tomorrow and we shall learn it. I am rather hoping it is Miss Sophiar (that is, Miss Ellis as I should now address her, being the eldest unmarried) or Miss Frunces. The younger sisters of

Mrs Muggins were such jolly company earlier in the summer but perhaps it will be a new acquaintance!

Aunt B has allowed me to have tea with the ladies every day of our visit, which is quite the social whirl compared to my usual routine.

Cousin Fordyce (the Colonel, not one of the other Fordyces, what a bore it is for so many of one's relatives to share the same handful of names, I once heard my brother referred to as the Other Fordyce which is quite inappropriate, and I simply can't call him Rackham like everyone else does, but he does frown so when I call him Ford in front of anyone who isn't family so it is 'brother' this and 'brother' that when we are in polite company) anyway, Cousin Fordyce is teaching me Claw, one of the many card games I have been informed will be useful to me once I am married and dull. What a thing to look forward to! Cousin F. wishes me to pass on his compliments and to say how much he enjoyed your conversations over supper. If only he were looking for a wife, I believe we could have you in the family in a snap! I am not sure why it is he can't have a wife as well as the army, but Ford says I must not ask such personal questions even of cousins, and I am still on my best behaviour as I do not want to risk losing even a minute of Quartz's proposed visit.

My brother sends his compliments also and hopes you are well.

Yours sincerely,
Miss Tatiana Rackham

DIMITY, SUCH NEWS, I *cannot contain myself.*

Please write to me in haste with <u>any</u> information you have about a Miss Laura Bellamy of Merrywist, [Something]—shire as I believe you became acquainted over the spring and it is <u>most</u> important that Quartz and I know EVERYTHING about her IMMEDIATELY

Tatiana

MY DEAR TATIANA,

I am alarmed to read the name of Miss Laura Bellamy in your recent letter. Is she the visitor that Mrs Muggins was expecting? I am all surprise as I would not have expected Miss Laura's mama to forgive Mrs Muggins quite so expediently.

You know I am not one to gossip, but I can perhaps share a little of the circumstances by which Mr and Mrs Muggins became engaged...

DIMITY, *your letter was terribly late and not the least useful. Why should I care to hear about Miss Laura's failure to become engaged to our curate when I clearly wished to hear any and all details about her acquaintance with my brother!!!*

She has now been at the rectory for six days, and has dined with us once (with another to come this evening), and has been invited to tea with Aunt Beautrice FIVE TIMES, and I don't know what to think about it all.

Did you know that her family were hunters? Quartz explained it to me, after a few veiled comments between Miss Bellamy and my aunt over currant biscuits.

My aunt has such an unfortunate fascination with young ladies from hunter families, she always thinks she can fix them, and I have heard the tale far too many times about how my Grandmama Tatiana stabbed three gold-backs in the neck before she was engaged to my Grandpapa (Fordyce, of course) and became the most dutiful Lady of Hoarders.

SEVERAL LINES CROSSED out on the best note paper:

~~My dear Tatiana~~
~~Dear Tatiana~~
~~It's all a great deal more complicated~~
~~I am not sure I know anything useful~~
~~WHAT IS HAPPENING?~~

~~Dear Tatiana~~

DEAR DIMITY

ALL IS SILENCE and I am <u>bereft</u>. We have returned to Malachite, and I hope to see you on the fourteenth as previously arranged.

I would love to explain the events of the last few days but in truth I understand little of it. Quartz appears to know more, and we had quite the fierce quarrel when she refused to share matters that I believe she witnessed.

In any case:

I believe my brother is in love with Miss Laura Bellamy.

I believe my brother may have PROPOSED MARRIAGE to Miss Laura Bellamy

I believe that Miss Laura has broken his heart.

We must discuss the events of the last few weeks in person as a matter of great urgency.

Your dear friend,
Miss Tatiana Rackham

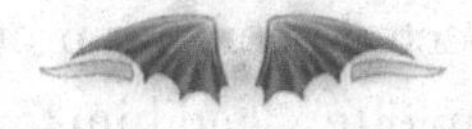

CHAPTER 16

IN LOVE WITH THE RACKHAMS

Of all the houses I have ever loved, there is none but Malachite which truly holds my soul. (One cannot, after all, properly fall in love with a rented house, no matter how fine.) Every corner of Malachite is dear to me, rich in memories and warm in welcome.

My favourite thing about the house is not the majesty of its grey stone pillars, the natural beauty of the exquisite grounds, or the comfort of the furnishings. It is that being here, on the estate or in the nearby village, one is surrounded by people who love Mr Rackham and his dear sister Tatiana as much as Chambrey and Dido and I always have.

In Abberline, while Mr Rackham is generally surrounded by respected peers, his proud nature and natural aloofness can often lead him to be misunderstood by new acquaintances (much as happened in Merrywist, where the lack of protection usually provided by his city reputation as a gentleman worth knowing had stark consequences).

In Malachite there is not a servant or villager above the age of five-and-twenty who does not remember Mr Rackham as the grave young boy who inherited so much responsibility in his twelfth year, including the baby sister he was left to protect even before they were also made motherless.

I believe old Mr Rackham was respected in this community — but he was an imposing man, all bark and eyebrows. I cannot imagine he was loved as our Mr Rackham is loved.

It frustrates him sometimes, I think, that every baker and brewer and all but the youngest of housemaids remember him as that boy, though he is now a grown man. But he never shows that frustration, except the occasional wince or sigh when none but the most attentive are observing him.

Taking care of others is a skill at which Mr Rackham excels, and everything about his home is designed for the comfort and convenience of residents, staff and guests. There is no new time-saving device that he will not invest in, to accommodate his servants; no village need that he does not predict and fund well ahead of time.

Then there is his aunt, who is always met with comfort and flawless service when she visits a few times per year.

Tatiana once told me that after each of Lady Beautrice's stays at Malachite, every servant who attended upon her was allotted an extra week off, to be used at any time during the remainder of the year. Mr Rackham has been known to time his trips to Abberline carefully, allowing the house staff to take their week all at once if they wish, in order to recover from his aunt's presence. One year, when Lady B visited a total of four times instead of the usual three, Tatiana got to see every museum in the city thanks to her brother whisking her away and closing up the house the second that Lady B had left the premises.

Malachite is a house built for dragons and humans: the entire ground floor was constructed with wide arched doorways and sturdy pillars, including a garden parlour, a sunken dining room and several guest suites around the courtyard. The upper floors, with their spiral staircases and more delicate fixings, were designed in an era when it was not considered insulting to build human retreats from serpentine patrons.

When Lady B or any of her dragon friends are in residence, all entertainments and meals are taken on the ground floor out of courtesy.

She never stays in the house itself. The genius architect behind the beauty and clever design of the Malachite estate added a separate dragon bower to the grounds, which I believe won him several awards (and the endless gratitude of the Rackham family).

Upon this occasion, Dido and I arrived at Malachite in the middle of the afternoon — Chambrey and Mr Harefield had come on a few days ahead of us, preferring to take the journey on horseback while we ladies rattled around in the chaise and four with plenty of space to bring Marjoram along with us.

Dido immediately went up to her room to rest. The gentlemen had not yet returned to the house from some day trip or other; we do not expect the usual niceties of proper greetings at Malachite, which is quite our home away from home.

A cheerful housemaid offered to fetch Miss Rackham to join me for tea, but I was happy to go hunting for the daughter of the house all on my own — with an impending visit from young Quartz, I knew exactly where I would find Tatiana.

They called it Carnelians Cottage, for no one ever stayed there but Lady B and her daughter. Several generations of the Rackham family had taken their aunt's exacting recommendations as to every tasteful furnishing or decoration so that it looked like a miniature version of her own home (only built in the same grey stone as Malachite, instead of the ruby red of Carnelians).

This lesser Carnelians was more of a temple than a cottage, all sturdy pillars and rounded walls with a larger portico wrapped around a cozy inner sanctum. Still, the name amused Lady B, and no one would change it while she lived.

The housekeeper of Malachite — Mrs Wrexham, a most competent and thoughtful woman — would have already arranged for the cottage to be scrubbed clean, restocked with dragon goodies and ready for its guest, but of course Tatiana would have her own touches to add now she was growing up and thinking of such things. Until Mr Rackham married, there was no other chatelaine at Malachite.

As I stepped into the bower in my travelling boots, the scent of fresh roses filled the air. Sunlight, filtered through scarlet stained-glass windows, cast a warmth upon the chilly grey of the stone. The swords mounted on the wall — family heirlooms, used in defence of the estate — gleamed also in the crimson-tinted light.

"Dimity!" cried Tatiana, turning from the enormous vase where she had been arranging bounty from the garden. "Does it not look perfect? Quartz has never been allowed to stay here on her own before. I want her to love it."

"Of course she'll love it," I assured her.

"I want her to feel comfortable!" the girl exclaimed. "Everyone says she'll soon be building a hoard of her own, and it won't be here, of course, but wouldn't it be fun if it was? Then she could live at Malachite always."

"Next generation dragons don't usually stay within the same family," I cautioned her, not wanting Tatiana to be disappointed if Quartz ran off with some other marriageable lass. "It's not the done thing."

Tatiana huffed. "I know that. Aunt Beautrice keeps hinting, though, that if Quartz bonds with a lady or gentleman who is *about* to marry into the family, then no one would be too offended."

"Yes," I said gravely, remembering how many times Lady B dropped hints over dinner that a future wife of her favourite nephew Mr Rackham would be fortunate indeed. "Not so much hints as enormous boulders dropped on the tea table." Poor Quartz would have to be very determined to evade the influence of her mother when it came to making the big decisions that were on her horizon.

Speaking of hints and boulders, I was rather desperate to know what Tatiana had to share about her brother's doings at Carnelians over the summer (I had read that last letter about Miss Laura Bellamy twelve times and it still made no sense in the least!), but I did not wish to appear too eager — we likely must wait for Quartz, in any case, to cut through to the truth.

"When does your house guest arrive?" I asked.

"Before supper, I hope!" Tatiana's eyes were alight. "It will be like a proper house party, with you both here."

Not at all like a proper house party, given the lack of eligible gentlemen to hurl myself at, but I had committed to attend three week-long gatherings elsewhere before the end of the summer, and thus could enjoy this sojourn at Malachite as a proper holiday, without the usual primping and fluttering.

"Surely you have visits with other friends to look forward to," I suggested. Mr Rackham might be a fearsome and protective guardian, but he must know that young ladies needed friends. Tatiana had never gone away to school, but he had often allowed her to be privately introduced to young ladies her own age, from suitable families, and she kept up a lively correspondence with many of them.

Now, Tatiana's face fell as I mentioned it. "Not this year," she said, with a hint of misery. "Not after what happened when I went to stay with Helena Baines last summer."

I could not think what she meant. The Baines family were respectable to the point of stuffy, and not the least lacking in decorum. Their dragon, Mrs Marylebone, was a pillar of the community in Chesterdyle, one of the western counties, as well as an elder matron of the Coterie. It had not surprised me last year to hear that Mr Rackham had allowed Tatiana to visit her friend without his own supervision given the sheer number of aunts known to reside at their country estate; it surprised me a great deal now that this freedom was no longer to be allowed.

I would have pressed further, but we both heard carriage wheels in that moment, screeching on the gravel drive with the kind of heavy tread one only gets when a dragon is inside said carriage.

"She's here!" squealed Tatiana, whipping out to see her friend.

THERE WAS no time to talk for the rest of the day. All was taken up with greetings and tea and more greetings, and supper, and so on. Finally, as Dido started to make noises about playing Claw, Tatiana suggested that she and I escort Quartz to the cottage, to ensure the young dragon was settled comfortably.

Mr Rackham seemed amused. "One hour," he said sternly. "Then bed, Tatiana. I am sure you will be up at dawn to plan all your amusements for the week."

His sister clapped her hands, smiling like sunshine.

Fierce protector he might be, but there was little Rackham would refuse her; it troubled me that something had happened last summer to inspire such drastic measures as restricting Tatiana's visits to playmates. No wonder she had seemed so starved for company when I first saw her at Carnelians.

A servant had already lit the flaming torches in the grey sanctum, which threw dramatic shadows against the walls as we followed Quartz in. There were family crests on the wall, I noticed — those of the de Bramble family as well as the Rackhams — alongside the heirloom swords.

My taste for gothic literature does mean I feel a delicious sort of shiver when I see a sword, even one of a decorative variety.

"My dears," said Quartz, pounding the flagstones with her clawed feet, where a scattering of ruby red beads popped brightly among the grey of her baby scales. "Has there been any word from the Bellamy?"

"Not a letter," said Tatiana immediately. "I've been checking my brother's post in and out."

"Tatiana!" I was a little shocked by her behaviour.

The girl shrugged unapologetically. "If Ford is going

to run around proposing to unsuitable girls without telling me about it, I must be ruthless."

There was something about hearing her say it out loud that made me dizzy; I had thought it outrageous enough when penned to the page. "You don't really think he proposed?"

"I do," said Quartz, her eyes gleaming. "I overheard him speaking in confidence to my mother. He *told* her he was planning to propose to someone, and soon. She didn't seem to approve — not exactly. She said: 'Are you sure about this young lady, Rackham?' And he said: 'I have never been more certain of anything.' Isn't that romantic?"

There must be something wrong with my stays. They felt over-tight. "It certainly sounds romantic," I allowed. "Did either of them mention Miss Laura? Are you sure she was the one he meant?"

"Oh no," Quartz said with a swish of her scaled tail that almost took out the giant flower arrangement. "This was before she arrived. I didn't even mention what I overheard to Tatiana, because I hadn't the faintest idea whom he meant to marry. But the very next day, *she* turned up as the guest of Mrs Muggins."

"That isn't the strange part," insisted Tatiana. "No, it was that Aunt Beautrice liked her."

Quartz nodded. "It was the most peculiar thing. Mama kept asking questions about the Bellamy family and Miss Laura would say terrible things, like how her father was a legendary hunter —" We all winced. "And all her sisters were out in society at once, all that sort of thing. But the more shocking she was, the more intrigued Mama became. She insisted that the Mugginses and their guest dine with us every night."

"She was constantly asking Miss Laura to play the piano," said Tatiana with a pout. "And asking her to tea in private. I asked my brother about it, and he seemed — concerned that Aunt B was taking such an interest. And then..." She looked at Quartz.

"I was practicing my flying," whispered the young dragon. "I saw him enter the rectory, when Miss Laura was the only one of the family at home. He stayed for at least thirty minutes. The only reason could possibly be that he went to find her alone, to propose to her. He left in such a temper and was quite stormy for the rest of the day. Everyone remarked upon it."

Tatiana nodded. "Ford refused to make conversation after supper. Instead, he sat down and wrote a letter which he later sent to the rectory. Then he insisted we make for home the next day, though we'd planned to stay three more nights. I asked why, but..."

I took a few deep breaths. I was the elder of the three. It was up to me to damp these fires before they became a more damaging kind of gossip. We must be sensible, even if it felt as if the world was ending. "It seems to me that nothing of any import has occurred," I said, forcing calm into my tone, and wishing above all things that I spoke the truth. "If it is true that Mr Rackham lost his head and proposed to an unsuitable young lady, well, we must be grateful that she was sensible enough to throw him over."

I could not understand why she would have refused

him — why any young lady, especially one with such an urgent need for a good marriage as a Bellamy sister, would not be delighted to have such a gentleman as her husband. Mr Rackham was hardly *Mr Muggins*. And why, having been thus rejected, would he write her a letter to mark the occasion?

Tatiana and Quartz stared at me, their eyes almost equally brimming with concern.

"If he loves her, and she does not love him, is that not terribly sad?" Tatiana asked.

"Gentlemen propose to the wrong lady all the time," I informed them. "And young ladies reject marriage proposals nearly as often. It does not always resolve itself as tidily as this matter has done. You should both forget everything you think you know. When Mr Rackham is truly to be married, he — and Lady Beautrice, probably — will make an announcement in the open, and there will not be the slightest doubt that he has made the correct choice."

If there was a hollow place inside me at the very thought of Mr Rackham loving a lady, and being unloved in return, then it was nobody's business but my own.

CHAPTER 17
ON THE MATTER OF MR FAIRBANKS

The little path that led from Carnelians Cottage to the back of the big house was lined with tiny lanterns, and so Tatiana and I could see perfectly well on our way back to the main house. I shooed her up the stairs in good time — a full ten minutes before I had promised to have her safely on her way to bed.

The door to the library cracked open as I passed the first landing; as in Elderflower Hall, it was generally this room where the family retired for company and cards after supper (at least, when one was not entertaining adult dragons, as the draughty Lower Parlour was available as a more inclusive alternative).

"You are good to spend so much time entertaining my sister," said Mr Rackham, drawing the door back for me and welcoming me into the warmth of the room.

The Malachite library is not quite so grand, I suppose, as the one at Elderflower Hall — it has not the height and unnecessary breadth better suited to a ball-room, but that only makes it a more inviting space. Every book on the shelves has been chosen with care, the carpets are thick, and the chairs wide enough to make space for more substantial gowns than are currently in fashion.

Both of my siblings had already retired for the night. Mr Harefield dozed by the fire with a newspaper folded over his chest; he would do as a chaperone.

"You know I enjoy Tatiana's company," I said in a tone that was only half-scolding. "It is a delight to play the elder sibling for once."

Mr Rackham poured me a generous glass of ratafia, an indulgence I occasionally enjoy if Dido is not there to give me haughty looks; it is usually Chambrey who pours it for me. "You are something of a hero to her, you know," he remarked.

"Goodness! I can't think why." Tatiana was at least twice as promising a young lady as I had been at the same age, and she had so many more advantages.

Mr Rackham gave me an odd sort of smile that suggested he knew exactly why, but was not going to tease me with further compliments. That was for the best. Compliments did not mix well with ratafia; too much of either would lead to reddened cheeks and an upset stomach.

In any case, we all knew that Tatiana's hero was her brother, not her brother's friend's twin sister.

We sat together in the warmth of the library, accompanied only by the gentle snores of my brother-in-law. I had matters I wished to discuss with Mr Rackham while we had this rare moment only to ourselves but was not entirely sure how to begin.

I hear you proposed marriage to my nemesis this summer was not the most genteel conversational gambit.

"Did you enjoy the rest of your stay at Carnelians?" I ventured, which should be safe enough.

Mr Rackham frowned. "There were a few unusual occurrences."

I tried not to look too eager to learn all about them. "Indeed?"

"Mrs Muggins had a house guest from Merrywist." He gave me a mildly suspicious expression which was only partly warranted. "But you knew that already."

I took pity on him. "Miss Laura made quite the impression on young Quartz, and your sister. I believe she may be a new favourite of Lady de Bramble?"

"My aunt has always had an eccentric taste for companions," said Mr Rackham darkly.

He did not seem especially heart-broken upon mentioning Miss Laura's name, which was a cheering development.

"Something is bothering you," I said. "Naturally, you do not have to tell me anything."

"No, I think I should." Rackham took a deep breath and stared at his hands. "The truth is, Dimity, there's something I should have told you a long time ago."

I felt a small shiver go through me. I had not been expecting a conversation of this gravity. "About Miss Laura?" I said in a small voice.

"No, not at all." He seemed surprised at the very idea. "About Tatiana."

I let out a small breath. "What's wrong with Tatiana?" My mind flitted back to the odd exchange I had shared with her earlier in the day. "Is this about her visit to the Baines family last summer?"

Mr Rackham's shoulders, usually so reliably upright, sagged a little. "Of course she told you."

"Hardly anything at all. I only wondered at her being so lonely this year." I hadn't meant to say that. "What happened last summer?"

Mr Rackham's gaze fixed upon mine. "Gideon Fairbanks happened," he said.

Oh, no.

IT COULD HAVE BEEN WORSE. Worse situations occurred to young ladies of good fortune all across the country with an alarming constancy. All it took was for the watchful eye of a guardian to slip for a moment. Some of these stories had far more sordid endings; others might even be resolved in a happy marriage, though it was hard to imagine how happy it could be, with a beginning like *that*.

Tatiana had been lucky.

But it had been so near a misadventure, I was

astounded Mr Rackham could bear to leave his sister's side for even a moment.

It went like this:

Tatiana, at fifteen years old, was staying at the home of her friend Miss Helena Baines in Chesterdyle. Neither of them was Out, so they were not allowed to attend dances or supper parties like Helena's two older sisters, but there were plenty of village entertainments to which young ladies might be included in all respectability.

Earlier that same summer, Gideon Fairbanks visited Malachite to ask Mr Rackham to purchase a commission on his behalf, so that he might enter the militia. He called upon the love that the old Mr Rackham had held for him as a boy, and the promise to sponsor him in the career of his choice.

Our Mr Rackham refused to supply further funds on the grounds that he had not only previously honoured his father's pledge to pay for Fairbanks' education, but that he had outlaid a great deal of money on him upon gradua-tion — firstly, to set him up as a curate with a living in a nearby village and then, after Fairbanks decided the ecclesiastical life did not suit him, a generous compen-satory settlement that should easily have provided a steady allowance for any young man whose tastes did not run to gambling and debauchery.

Further financial support was, in Mr Rackham's eyes, wholly unnecessary.

Gideon Fairbanks was not a person to be easily thwarted. Within weeks of Mr Rackham's refusal, he had joined a party of merrymakers in Chesterdyle, where he finagled an introduction to the Baines family under the guise of courting their eldest daughter. From there, he managed to arrange discreet "accidental" encounters with young Miss Rackham, often enough to convince her that they were in love.

Poor Tatiana, bright-eyed and paid attention to by a handsome suitor for the first time, swiftly found herself on the verge of an elopement. At the last minute, she decided she must be honest with her brother before leaving, sending him a letter that revealed all.

Rackham rode through the night, saved her from scandal, and wrote out a bank note to sponsor Fairbanks for the militia on condition he never speak to a member of the family again. He had been agonising over the matter ever since.

My heart broke for them both upon learning all this. At the same time, I was overwhelmed with the desire to scold Mr Rackham (ever so slightly).

"I see from your face you have opinions," he said after a long silence. I often used to think he had the sort of face which would not be truly handsome until he is older; there was a strong-featured shape about his nose and brow that did not seem quite suited to a man in his twenties, but would make all the sense in the world once there was a portrait on the wall of him at forty years old, gazing over all that he surveys.

In the firelight, I could see that I was entirely wrong. There was no one whose face I would rather look upon in this moment.

My mouth was a little dry, but I managed to speak. "Mr Rackham, when have you ever known me *not* to have opinions?"

He spread his hands wide. "How, then, have I handled things all wrong?"

"I did not say that, either," I said, with a hint of tetchiness. "But isolation is not protection. You were clearly let down by the Baines family, who should have kept a closer eye on Tatiana. But you were not at fault for letting her spend time in company with friends her own age. You have so many people who might love and protect your sister. You have your Aunt Beautrice and Quartz. You have Dido and I, and Chambrey. How is it that you feel you must be parent and brother all on your own?"

THERE WAS further silence between us after that, though I like to think it was not especially awkward.

"Does Dido know about the matter of Mr Fairbanks?" I asked, nursing my final sip of ratafia in case it was needed.

"Only Chambrey, whom I confided in after Fairbanks

turned up at Merrywist. A few members of the Baines family, who are sworn to secrecy. And…" There, Mr Rackham's face took on an odd, rarely-seen expression. "I told Miss Laura Bellamy," he confessed.

I swallowed the final sip of ratafia faster than lightning. "*What*? When?" Why on earth would he trust such a viper with a family secret of such delicacy? Tatiana could still be ruined if the story escaped years after the event.

"It was an accident."

"Mr Rackham," I said in a stern voice. "I have never known you to say anything without due consideration. How could you accidentally…" My mind was racing. Of course he would. If he thought what happened to Tatiana might happen to another young lady. Had he not attempted to, rather discreetly, use me for such a purpose back at Merrywist? If anything, he had been too discreet. My own conflicts with the Bellamy family meant that the message was never properly delivered.

If Rackham was more invested in the fortunes of the Bellamy family than anyone might suppose, then of course he would wish to ensure they were protected from a fortune hunter like Mr Fairbanks… "Did you propose to her?" I blurted out.

Now Rackham looked horrified. "To Miss Laura? With *that* mother?"

I was not sure whether to laugh or cry. "Tatiana thinks you did."

"Tatiana, as established, knows very little of the world!"

I took a deep breath and stared into my empty ratafia glass. "So, you did not."

"No. Even if I did, believe me, I am the last gentleman whom Miss Laura Bellamy would condescend to marry. She made sure I was thoroughly aware of that fact."

"But you did not propose in the first place."

"I did not."

We were both breathing rather rapidly. I had so many questions, and no right to ask any of them. "You spoke to her in private," I murmured. "At the rectory."

"How the devil do you know that?" His eyes narrowed. "Quartz."

"The girls were not gossiping," I said immediately.

"Were they not?"

I gave him a rather plaintive look, and Mr Rackham relented.

"I had no intention of seeking a private audience with Miss Laura," he assured me. "I was hoping to speak with her in the company of Mrs Muggins in order to pass on my concerns about Gideon Fairbanks. I had heard her speak of him several times while ingratiating herself with my aunt, and when she mentioned that her youngest sister was going to the seaside in company of several senior wives of the militia..."

I winced. The youngest Bellamy girl, the same age as Tatiana. "I see."

"It did not go well."

"Your advice was not appreciated?"

"It was not heard," he said, with some frustration. "In

the course of her many teas at Carnelians, Miss Laura had shared some conversation with my cousin Fordyce, who was — like my aunt — under the impression that I wished to court the young lady. His intention to make me appear a worthy gentleman hinged rather on a particular anecdote about my role in saving a good friend from an unworthy marriage." He gave me a weary expression.

I winced. "That's my fault." In conversation with Colonel Fordyce, I had certainly brought up an edited tale of the Rescue of Chambrey Iverwold, giving Rackham perhaps more credit than he was due. It was Colonel Fordyce's greatest entertainment in life to hear his cousin praised.

"I thought it might be," said Rackham, with a startling lack of rancour. "In any case, Miss Laura was primed to boil over in fury at me when I called upon her, and given the unfortunate nature of the timing... with Mrs Muggins not at home to chaperone... and added to it all, the impression given to Miss Laura by both my cousin and my aunt that I might be on the verge of proposing... let us say that it was a conversation in which little of any substance was conveyed between us."

A blinding row, in other words. How the servants must have enjoyed it!

"The whole thing was rather embarrassing," he added.

"I can imagine."

"It was clear to me as I withdrew that Miss Laura still thought highly of Mr Fairbanks. On reflection afterwards,

I came to believe that she might be in as great danger as her sister from his machinations."

I blinked. "It did not occur to you that in such an instance, Miss Laura was the person most likely to murder Mr Fairbanks on the spot?"

Mr Rackham huffed a laugh. "I was frustrated and wrapped up in my own failures. Before I could stop myself I wrote a rather foolhardy letter in an attempt to clarify matters between myself and Miss Laura."

I paled. "You wrote of Tatiana's situation in a letter?"

"It seemed a matter of urgency that Miss Laura be aware that my only intentions in speaking to her came from concern for her family..."

I had certainly missed something. "Does *Miss Laura* think you proposed marriage to her?"

"I cannot see how she would have got such an impression," Mr Rackham said stiffly. "And yet, in our exchange of words... as I ran over them in my head afterwards, it became clear that she felt the need to refuse a proposal I had never made."

Oh, what a pickle.

"But, yes," he went on. "I did indeed give the shape of Tatiana's situation in that letter. It has occurred to me in the days since that it was a great deal of intimacy to share with a person with whom I do not intend any further conversation."

My mind was racing. Perhaps I could speak to Leda, to request the letter be returned.

"It seems unlikely that Miss Laura would wish anyone to read a piece of correspondence in which the author made it clear he had never proposed to her," I murmured.

"Indeed," Mr Rackham said heavily. "I have no particular fear that Miss Laura will use it for ill. But afterwards, all I could think was that — it felt deeply inappropriate that a near-stranger had been apprised of such a significant family matter when I had never told *you* the truth of it."

Oh, that.

"I would not let you," I said, remembering a day in Merrywist when Mr Rackham teetered on the brink of a confession about Gideon Fairbanks. "I told you I would not ask. Everyone deserves their secrets."

"I spoke to Tatiana when we returned home," he replied. "Apologised for sharing a matter that concerned her reputation far more than my own. She urged me to tell you all, on her behalf."

A breath of a laugh crossed my lips. "You cannot have explained the circumstances properly. She is still determined to believe you proposed marriage to a certain person."

Rackham laughed, too, a rare sight: his eyes creased up and I thought all over again that he was the person I most liked to look upon, by firelight or otherwise.

Most importantly of all, comic and tragic misunderstandings aside, *he had not proposed to Laura Bellamy*.

(Still, I recalled, he had informed his aunt that he intended to propose to someone. If not Laura Bellamy, then who?)

CHAPTER 18
A HOARD AT MALACHITE

On the third day of my stay at Malachite, I discovered that a strand of pearls had gone missing from my room. The culprit was hardly difficult to locate; in the course of her meanderings, she had also swept several ornaments off the dresser and left one clear claw mark on the carpet.

I emerged from my room to meet Tatiana on the landing, her eyes wide with excitement. "Have you anything missing?" she demanded, giggling behind her hands. "I have lost three rings and the polished brass knobs from the end of my bed!"

"Have you indeed?" I said, matching her enthusiasm with my own. "Come along, the hunt is on!"

Our investigation through the house turned up several more missing items: half a pair of cufflinks from Chambrey, a set of bronze book ends from Mr Rackham, and a watch-chain from Mr Harefield.

Dido was disappointed that her own dresser had not

been ransacked; she tipped a handful of old brooches into my hands in case they would be useful when we cornered the criminal. "I'm not so formidable as all that, am I?" she lamented.

I chose not to answer the question honestly; what lady would do otherwise?

The maids reported several silver teaspoons missing, and one of them giggled over a platinum sugar bowl that had been emptied neatly on to a tea tray before being snatched.

Everyone was in on the joke; glee danced from one end of the household to the other.

Nothing was more splendid or honourable than to witness the gathering of a dragon's first hoard.

WE DID NOT HAVE to look very hard to find her. Quartz was not in Carnelians Cottage, but from its portico we could see the trail where she had slid over the gentle hillside towards the river.

"She has a perfectly good cellar beneath a trapdoor at the cottage," Tatiana complained. "I made sure Millie dusted it, just in case."

"She may have gone a little wild," I observed. "It does happen, you know!" There were so many tales about the scrapes young dragons got into, once the urge to hoard fell upon them.

"Come, Rackham!" called Chambrey, bouncing on his heels and quite as excited as Tatiana. "Will you not join us?"

Mr Rackham smiled with his eyes as he stood at the back porch, with several of the staff clustered around in curiosity. "I do not wish to crowd my cousin. She's only young. I trust Mr Iverwold to ensure you don't all end up in the water." I fancied he gave me a particularly pointed look, which was wholly unnecessary.

We located Quartz at the muddiest part of the river, her scales rosy and her eyes glazed with delight; it took only a little convincing that the cottage would be safer and easier to defend, and a little more convincing for her to allow us to tote her treasures on her behalf, so that she needn't try to carry them all in her mouth, or wound around her claws.

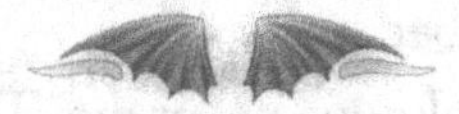

Quartz's hoard was to be the theme of our summer. She could not continue to steal trinkets entirely from the household. We did not mind, but it was hardly a sustainable enterprise.

It was Chambrey who suggested we take a tour of the surrounding villages; it was considered lucky for any place to donate a token to a growing hoard, and at Scales Landing there was soon to be a fete which meant good things to eat as well as the potential for a few extra shinies.

One did not expect a new dragon's hoard to be made entirely of gold and jewels; not at first, and not in this day and age where conquest was rather looked down upon. Once Quartz fully came into her colour, there would be jewels aplenty; she could go caving for raw materials, and then there would be courting gifts as the nobles of Abberline and high society competed for her favour.

There were all manner of magical dragon secrets which humans — even old hoarding families like mine and the Rackhams — were never allowed to share. Lady Beautrice de Bramble sat upon a hoard of uncut rubies, for instance, that had never seen the light of day. Had she scrabbled them all out of caves with her claws? Had she stolen them from pirates? Snatched them out of thin air? No one in the Rackham family had the faintest idea, nor did they expect her to tell them, unless she was feeling chatty on her deathbed.

(Dragons, as we know, never die. They merely sleep as statues until they no longer wish to wake. No deathbed confessions for them; all the better to preserve their secrets.)

Tatiana was beside herself with joy at this new development; there were now daily outings and amusements, and as our various parties consisted of close family and friends, being Out or not was no particular concern.

A lady does not have to have been presented at Court to escort her dragon friend from village to village, as long as she is properly chaperoned.

Chambrey took great joy in planning every visit on our behalf. Even Mr Harefield got in on the fun, enjoying the outings as much as he ever admits to enjoying anything.

Mr Rackham mostly watched from afar, but his expression was generally warm as he observed Tatiana's joy. He occasionally joined us on our adventures, but more often stayed at home to attend to estate matters, trusting in Dido and me — and Chambrey, and Mr Harefield, and Quartz — to keep Tatiana safe from harm.

All hoarding families know that when dragons begin their work, hunters are never far behind, even in these enlightened times.

WHEN THE DAY of the Scales Landing fete arrived, we had already visited seven other villages. Quartz was something of a local celebrity.

Upon our arrival on the green, several children ran up to present garlands of flowers for Quartz to wear, which made her blush ruby-red across the sculpted planes of her face.

Scales Landing, as its name suggested, was a village founded by dragons rather than humans. There were several local aunts and patrons in attendance at the fete, who treated Quartz with amiable condescension.

Not a thatched roof in sight, which was a sensible

precaution with so many dragons in the vicinity; slate is not nearly as combustible.

The Malachite party arrived in two carriages and a hay cart, allowing space aplenty of the maids and footmen of the house, as it was their half-day, and everyone loves a fete. Rackham, Chambrey and Mr Harefield all rode horseback to leave more spaces for seating the servants.

It was a lovely day, all sunshine and sweetmeats and playing the tombola and lawn games. In the centre of it all: Quartz, queen of the fete, with every villager from the eldest to the youngest contributing some small item (a hand-made dolly or twist of wire or copper penny) to her new hoard, trusting that the gift would bring them fortune, and that it never hurt to have a dragon in your debt.

A hoard, after all, might last for centuries, and that penny could still be bringing luck to your family eight generations from now.

(Chambrey and Mr Harefield made sure to distribute small gifts and coins to the villagers so that they were not left impoverished by our visit; Mr Rackham had stocked up on silver sixpences especially for today, knowing how many folk would be in attendance.)

Tatiana and I were quite giddy with it all.

Quartz glowed under the attention.

Naturally, part way through the most pleasant afternoon of the summer, Mr Rackham felt it was time for himself to withdraw. I followed him to his horse, attempting to convince him that the world would not end if he allowed himself a little more pleasure.

"Will you not stay for the bonfires?" I wheedled.

"Strictly speaking," he said with an expression that was not the least stern, as a day of relaxation had quite smoothed out his brow. "I should take Tatiana back with me now. And the maids."

"But you will not," I said, unable to hide my delight. "Because you trust Mrs Harefield and me to be the best and most responsible of chaperones."

"I trust you all," he agreed, glancing over my shoulder to where Tatiana and Quartz were at the see-saw, attempting to see how many of the village children it took to balance out the weight of even a medium-small dragon. "But I do have work to do, Dimity."

"We will allow it," I conceded, doing my best impersonation of Lady Beautrice de Bramble. "If we must."

Rackham paused with one hand on his bridle. "Do you think — there are no village visits planned for tomorrow, are they?"

"Chambrey insisted on a day of rest," I said. "It is

coloured in violet pastels on his most comprehensive schedule."

Rackham nodded. "Would you join me for a walk tomorrow? Before tea, perhaps. If you are not otherwise engaged with the youngsters."

"That would be lovely," I said, not even allowing the suggestion to run entirely through my head before I agreed. We had often walked together, Rackham and I, a general perambulation about the estate if we happened to feel like light exercise at the same time.

This was the first time he had ever made an appointment for my company.

His face broke into a warm smile. It was really quite astonishing I ever thought him less than handsome. Direct sunlight was quite as bad as firelight for making people's faces attractive to look upon. "Tomorrow, then," he murmured.

I watched him ride away, wondering what on earth was going on with him.

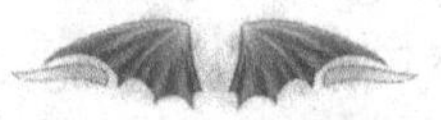

At that very moment, none of us even suspected that Laura Bellamy might be standing on the grounds of Malachite, taking in the splendours of the estate with the covetous gaze of a hunter.

CHAPTER 19
MR RACKHAM IS SURPRISED; MR TVERWOLD IS SURPRISING

We must not blame Mrs Wrexham. It is quite the usual arrangement for a housekeeper to accept a coin or two in exchange for showing strangers around a house as fine as Malachite, as long as the family is away and are unlikely to be disturbed.

Accompanied as she was by her (human) Aunt Gracechurch of Gardiner Street, Miss Laura Bellamy appeared to be an entirely respectable visitor with no motive other than mild curiosity about the grand home belonging to the Rackham family.

Given the respectability of this dainty elder lady and her niece, we should utter no reproach that, when asked about the splendid little temple behind the house, Mrs Wrexham shared the merry anecdote about the visiting dragon coming into her colour, as an explanation as to why visitors were not currently invited to admire the private sanctum of Carnelians Cottage.

The entire matter was so entirely beyond suspicion

that it is possible we might never have heard it happened at all, except that while her aunt exchanged recipes with the housekeeper, Miss Laura went wandering on the grounds towards the river, and happened across the newly-returned Mr Rackham — a gentleman whom, she now knew, had never intended to propose marriage to her, despite her violent rejection of said proposal.

Certainly I, as a guest of the family, should never have heard a word about it, had the matter ended there.

But nothing is simple or respectable or *discreet* where a Bellamy is concerned.

WE RETURNED BEFORE THE BONFIRES.

It was not even early evening yet, but a local chapter of the militia had arrived to join the merriment, and Tatiana went quite pale at the sight of all of those gold-trimmed flamecoats.

Quartz immediately claimed a stomach-ache from too much treacle toffee, making me suspect that she knew at least as much about the Matter of Gideon Fairbanks as Mr Rackham had confessed to me.

Dido leaped upon our excuses with relief, (she had been eying the soldiers with great suspicion), and immediately collected all of the maids to return with us. Chambrey volunteered to escort us in the carriages, leaving Mr

Harefield to supervise the later return of the male household staff by means of the haycart.

It was arranged easily enough, and we arrived back at Malachite well before dusk.

Tatiana and Dido went inside with the maids to report to Mrs Wrexham and let her know how many for supper. Chambrey and I escorted Quartz (whose stomach was now perfectly well) back to Carnelians Cottage.

Thus it was that we had a rather direct view of Mr Rackham, fully dressed and dripping wet, as he strode over the hillside in the direction of the house.

"Rackham, what the devil happened to you?" shouted my brother, demonstrating a marked absence of decorum.

Quartz and I stopped short, staring with wide eyes.

It is a strange thing, that a gentleman's shirt should be quite so transparent when wetted, and that the rest of his attire should appear rather more close-fitting than when dry. Not that such a thing happens often enough in polite society for it to be dwelled upon. A sudden rainfall, perhaps, might account for this particular instance, except that the sky had been clear all day.

There was a simpler explanation.

"Did you fall in the river?" I asked in astonishment.

Mr Rackham's face closed over, turning his gaze away as if he must imagine us elsewhere in order to proceed. "Iverwold, join me in my study when you have a moment," he said stiffly. "Miss Iverwold, Cousin Quartz... I would thank you to forget that you saw me under such circumstances."

Quartz and I, trained in the proper courtesies, bobbed our heads silently to acknowledge his request.

Mr Rackham strode towards the house, dripping wet, head held high.

The three of us remained quite frozen on the spot, staring after him.

Once Mr Rackham had disappeared inside the house, Chambrey let out a low whistle. "Did he fall or was he pushed?"

"What a ridiculous thing to say," I snapped back. "Who would have the temerity to push Mr Rackham into a river?"

Who, indeed, would have the motive? Everyone at Malachite loved its master.

After supper that evening -- with only myself, Tatiana, Dido and Quartz at the table, while Chambrey and Rackham remained closeted in Rackham's study — the gentlemen finally condescended to join us in the draughty, dragon-friendly Lower Parlour.

Mr Harefield had finally returned, smelling of beer and bonfire smoke, and promptly fell asleep in front of the fire.

Tatiana and Quartz were engrossed in some complex attempt to build a castle out of playing cards, a task made doubly difficult by the regular snorts of warm steam gusting from Quartz's snoot (which was, by now, quite overtaken by ruby-and-rose scales with only a smattering of grey remaining)

Short of players for Claw or any other common evening pastime, Dido and I were playing our own game of pretending we were both going to make progress on our respective embroidery projects without actually threading a needle.

Mr Rackham and Chambrey entered the room, making light conversation about the day's amusements, and the plans for the next week.

I was working very hard to do as Mr Rackham had requested and forget our earlier encounter. However, when one has spent one's entire existence *not* witnessing handsome men soaked through their clothes, it is more of a challenge than one might expect, to mentally erase the singular instance of it happening before one's eyes.

Chambrey made several cheerful remarks which failed to resolve into conversations. He began to dart glances in mine and Dido's direction in something approaching despair.

To our surprise, it was Mr Rackham who finally spoke, broaching the awkwardness of our party.

"I happened to meet Miss Bellamy this afternoon. Quite the surprise encounter."

Dido set down her embroidery frame with more of a clatter than the statement warranted. "Where?" she inquired, her eyes narrowing sharply. "When?"

"In the park."

"Here at *Malachite*?"

Rackham tilted his head, as if he had not expected the interrogation to come from these quarters. Chambrey looked amused, which I took to mean he already knew the particulars.

"Pray, which Miss Bellamy do you mean?" I broke in, already suspecting that it was not the option I would have preferred. Mr Rackham's ears had become the most extraordinary russet colour, and I knew that it was not Miss Leda who could possibly have had such an effect on him.

"Miss Laura," said Rackham with a slight frown, as if it had not occurred to him to specify.

I caught the strangest look on Chambrey's face; a darting awareness as he glanced back towards our sister. In that moment, I *knew*.

Chambrey was perfectly aware of our machinations to keep him away from Leda Bellamy. Perhaps he had been, all along. This realisation was so overwhelming that I was briefly distracted away from Mr Rackham's jaw-dropping revelation that Laura Bellamy had been here at Malachite.

Dido, comforted falsely by her own assumption that Leda Bellamy was the only sister we had to worry about, picked up her embroidery again, poking at the stitches with a fingernail. "What on earth was that young lady doing here? Plotting to break Dimity's leg in retaliation?"

"Not exactly," said Mr Rackham, glancing at myself and at Quartz, embarrassment evident on his face.

I had a sudden, startling vision of Miss Laura Bellamy pushing him into the river.

"She is travelling with her aunt, who was curious to see the house," he went on. "Mrs Wrexham believed us to be out all day, and so she allowed the visitors."

Dido sniffed. "It is a strange thing, for ordinary people to be so curious about another person's home." As if she herself did not spend half her life being delighted when invited to a grand manor she had not previously visited. "Was the wretched girl polite, at least, when faced with the master of Malachite?"

Chambrey silently went to the sideboard to pour Rackham a glass of whiskey.

Rackham gave Dido an exhausted sort of smile. "I think that our mutual surprise quite overtook the need for cordiality. I do not expect she shall visit again."

"Let us hope not, for her sake," I said tartly, breaking the rules of my own game to stab my embroidery with a perfectly-threaded needle. "Malachite has so *many* staircases."

Rackham's eyes met mine, and he gave me a wry nod; he was amused now, instead of embarrassed.

Perhaps I should utter veiled threats in his hearing more often, if it cheered him so.

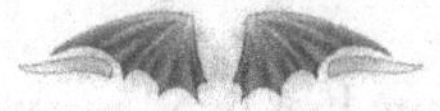

MR RACKHAM and I did not take that walk together, the following day. He apologised in that rather short way he often has about him when distracted by business.

I did not take it personally. Being pushed into a river by a Bellamy was bound to cause all manner of confusing thoughts in one's head.

Instead, I abducted my brother and insisted he perambulate to the village and back, to keep me company.

Chambrey agreed with all amiability, though I was certain he knew he had given himself away the night before and was fully prepared for my interrogation.

"So," I said to him as we turned into a pretty lane lined with hedges and wildflowers.

"So," he replied with a sunny smile.

"You are a wretch and a rascal, Chambrey Iverwold."

"And you, sister dear, are a conniving mistress of schemes."

I preened a little, rather liking that description. "If you say so."

"That was not a compliment," he added, digging me in the ribs with a finger.

I smacked his hand away. "You knew all along that Dido was desperately trying to keep you away from Leda Bellamy."

"If I didn't, you just failed in your scheme by admitting the particulars," he teased.

"You knew."

"Of course I knew. I've lived my whole life with you on one side of me and Dido on the other. Did you honestly think you could both develop all those feminine wiles without your brother building some minor defences against them?"

The lane was still empty of anyone but us; I kicked his ankle.

He pinched my arm and smirked down at me. "Do that again, Dimmy, and I'll throw your bonnet in a ditch."

"Did you know that she tried to call upon us in Abberline?"

"I know that you two shrews took her to a tea shop to keep her from seeing me," Chambrey replied. "And that Rackham was your co-conspirator — I usually have to drag him to the club, but there he was suggesting all manner of social outings without prompt. Of course there was plotting afoot. Besides," he added with a smile that others might consider winning. "The matter of Miss Laura's 'broken leg' at our ball was a dramatic enough piece of gossip that it made it to Abberline within days of our return. That you and Dido took tea with her sister only a few weeks later was reported on by all manner of society dragons. I heard it from several different sources before I joined you for supper that same day."

Drat the city. How had my friends not informed me that the tale of Miss Bellamy's leg was so well-known in society? No one had ever asked me about it! Had I made myself notorious?

"You're not cross at us?" I asked in a small voice. "Standing in the way of true love and all that?"

Chambrey scoffed. "Miss Leda is a jolly young lady, and I'm sure she'll make any worthy gentleman happy. But I've already told you that I'm not in the market for a wife. Perhaps if Rackham abandons bachelorhood, I might revisit the notion."

I was not accustomed to hearing my brother say so many sensible things in a row; it quite silenced me.

After a little more walking, my brother spoke again, his voice more serious than before. "I was prepared, you know, for what would happen when I came into my fortune. Rackham warned me that I would be surrounded by a sea of young ladies, hurled at me by their mamas, and that I must be careful not to make any sudden movements or I might catch one I did not wish to keep."

"I suppose the same thing happened to him," I mused. Rackham had twice Chambrey's fortune, and not even in trust; Old Mr Rackham had ensured his son would have control of the purse strings long before he came of age.

"Worse for him," snorted Chambrey. "I rather think that's why he allowed me his friendship; most of the chaps he was at school with were pressured by their aunts and patrons into flinging sisters and cousins at him. He'd had three attempts to trap him into compromising a young lady before he even left school, and he gave up on all social events at university after one of the Governors threatened to fail one of his exams if Rackham didn't agree to a pair of dances with the fellow's great-niece."

"I never knew any of that," I wondered.

"No reason why you should." Chambrey gave me a covert sort of look. "It eased off once he let it be known that Lady B had to approve of his bride. A few years ago, I helped him spread a rumour that the dragon clause was a codicil in the old man's will."

"Smart," I observed.

"I have my moments."

I squeezed his arm, and we returned to our walk with a more companionable air.

"Wait," I said, after a few moments of thought. "Why did you not *tell* Dido that you had no serious interest in courting dear Leda? Our sister is convinced she has pulled off some grand plot to separate you."

Chambrey looked wistful. "Exactly."

"I don't understand."

"Maybe *I'm* the one with wily machinations, leaving the two of you in the dark."

"Bonnet or no bonnet, darling brother, I am prepared to kick you again."

He sighed and patted my arm. "Do you not think that Dido has been rather lonely of late?"

I had not thought such a thing at all. "We've been so busy."

Busy creating distractions for a mildly heart-broken brother whom, it appeared, had not been in the least need of it.

Chambrey raised his eyebrows at me.

"Oh," I breathed. "You are the *devil*."

"Finally, acknowledgement of my genius."

Now that I came to think of it, the most recent winter had involved rather more Dido at home than in previous years. I was used to having to compete with her close circle of friends for her attention, but now they were all married and busily having babies, the letters and visits came less often, and...

I stopped still in the lane. "Chambrey. Does Dido want a baby?"

She had been married eight years. I was so young when she first married, I assumed it was good fortune that she had not been blessed in those early years, since she still had Chambrey and I to manage. Later... well, Dido showed no particular wistfulness when knitting booties for her friends. Two of her closest circle were married not long after she was, and now had several children to dote upon.

Lady Matilda Wapping, Dido's dearest childhood friend, had been a cheerful spinster until only two years ago when she was swept off her feet by a gentleman three years her junior. She had a baby in her arms within the year, and another born this summer...

"I don't know if Dido wants a baby particularly," Chambrey admitted. "But it is hard on her that all her friends are mothers, and she is not. Rather like they were all invited to the same assembly ball without her. She seemed... subdued, after learning that Lady Matilda was expecting her second."

"Am I a terrible sister for not noticing?"

"I prefer to say that *I* am an exceptional brother for noticing."

Once more, I was overcome with the desire to kick.

"You did not ship us to Elderflower Hall because of Dido, did you?"

"Not at all," Chambrey assured me. "I was being exactly as selfish as I previously confessed. But my interest in Miss Bellamy did seem to give Dido something to thwart... especially after that whole tea shop business, which cheered her for weeks. Pulling one over on me seems to have done her the world of good."

I began to walk again; Chambrey hurried after me.

"Are you cross that I did not confess earlier?" he asked.

"On the contrary. I am delighted to learn you are more devious than I previously suspected. Now perhaps I can stop worrying that you will..."

"Dimity." He twisted his arm into mine again. "As if I would marry someone you did not like."

He would never know what a relief it was to hear that from his lips. I was a fool. I should have spoken to him about all this months ago. "That's good to hear," I murmured.

"If I did find someone I wished to marry, I would certainly convince you to befriend her first, and perhaps even let Dido believe she was responsible for the match so that we could all be happy about it at the same time."

I blinked several times. To think I had imagined that Chambrey and I had grown apart as we left childhood behind.

Instead, he had learned to hide his scheming nature behind an open face.

"I don't know whether to be furious at you, or terribly proud," I said finally.

"Ah," said my brother, delighted with himself. "Wait until you figure out what I have been scheming on *your* behalf. It's going to be marvellous."

CHAPTER 20

SNUFFLING FOR SAPPHIRES

The next day, Tatiana and I came down to breakfast to find Dido waiting for us with a plate of pastries and preserves in front of her. This was quite an extraordinary happenstance, as the convention for married ladies to take a tray in their rooms was a privilege to which Dido was deeply devoted and would under normal circumstances guard with her life.

It was even more peculiar that Chambrey was not in attendance, as he would usually be on his third helping of breakfast by the time I reached for my first buttered roll.

Before Dido could explain, Quartz entered the breakfast room, arrowing towards the place setting specially arranged for her, already stacked with several pounds of braised steak and eggs that had been carried in by footmen the moment that her approach to the house was spotted from the kitchen windows. (A buffet table is not a convenient arrangement for dragons.)

"I saw Cousin Rackham and the other gentlemen

busy at the stables," Quartz noted, chewing on her first mouthful of the day, and nodding in polite thanks at Dido for filling her large saucer of tea. "Is this some new arrangement? I thought we were to visit Fife-on-the-Wold this afternoon."

Fife-on-the-Wold was a town that we had not previously planned to include in our lucky dragon tour because it was more than an hour away by carriage, but their mayor had written to the Rackhams with an open invitation for the family and house guests to admire a new fountain and bestow any dragon-related fortune that might be available.

"Mr Rackham has been called away," said Dido primly. "He requested the assistance of our brother, Mr Harefield, and several of the male servants as a matter of some urgency."

"What on earth can have happened?" Tatiana wondered aloud in the tone of one who is not terribly interested in the answer to her question

"I have no idea," said Dido in a low, terrible voice, her eyes fastened on me. "Chambrey seemed to think that you, Dimity, would be able to explain."

"I haven't the faintest," I began, but it was terribly hard to finish a sentence when Dido was staring at me as if I had drowned a kitten in front of her. "What can you mean?"

Surely Chambrey had not unleashed another scheme upon us all. I was already discombobulated by his recent revelations.

"The gentlemen of our household," Dido went on.

"Have left on some form of adventure to assist Mr and Mrs Gracechurch and the Bellamy family with a private emergency concerning the elopement of Miss Laura's youngest sister with a certain Mr Fairbanks." She said that last in quite a fierce tone.

Tatiana dropped her teacup. Quartz went to her side immediately, leaning into her. Tatiana mopped her lap, burst into tears, and left the morning room in a flurry with the dragon following close on her heels.

Dido's eyes went wide, as if she had not realised her wild stab would harm anyone but me. "Dimity, what on earth is happening in this house? And why was I the last to learn of it?"

My own thoughts were racing. All of them, Rackham and Chambrey and Mr Harefield, gone scampering after Laura Bellamy to save the day.

All she had to do was crook her finger.

"Was she here?" I asked finally. "Did Miss Laura actually come to this house to request Rackham's assistance?"

"No," said Dido, staring oddly at me. "He walked down to the village early to return a shawl or some such that Mrs Gracechurch left behind during their visit. He then stormed back in a froth of excitement, mustered the troops and left... Dimity, why are you crying? You never cry."

"I'm not crying," I insisted, mopping my overwrought face with a napkin. "I am merely concerned."

"*Concerned?*" Dido replied at her highest haught. "With Chambrey about to be dragged back into the web of that family? I should say you are concerned! If he does not return to us engaged, it will be a miracle."

"No," I said, mopping my face for a second time. My eyes continued to be overwrought to quite an alarming degree. "No, Dido, don't you see? Chambrey's not the one in danger. He was never the one who needed to be protected."

OUR GENTLEMEN DID NOT RETURN to Malachite that night. I went to bed in a state of extreme anxiety, convinced that something terrible was going to happen, far from here, where I could do nothing to stop it.

A duel. An engagement. Perhaps both at once.

I was a fool to think so. When the terrible thing happened, it was right here, at Malachite.

I WAS awoken a few hours before dawn by the warm breath of a dragon huffing in my face. My eyes flew open, and I stared at the head of Quartz, now thoroughly covered in scales of dark rose and ruby red.

Only her head, hovering just beneath the canopy of my four-poster bed, glowing strangely.

Another lady might have swooned or screamed; I was tempted to do both, but my curiosity fought all other impulses to a standstill.

"What?" I said, unprepared to put a more complex question together under the circumstances. "*What?*"

"Come through," Quartz said, pulling her head back into a glowing circle that I could now see was the fully illuminated inner sanctum of Carnelians Cottage. "Please, Dimity! I must tell someone."

The promise of gossip that no one else had heard overcame my good sense, and I leaned towards the light. With a swipe of her wing, Quartz pulled me through the opening in the air. I felt a flash of heat like that from a blazing hearth, and then I stumbled on to the flagstones of her sanctum in my white flannel nightgown.

"Can all dragons do that?" I demanded, whirling around. I caught a brief glimpse of the tasteful furnishings of my room before the circle closed and disappeared.

"It's one of our magical secrets," said Quartz. "Look at my tail, Dimity!"

Yesterday, her tail had been almost completely grey with only a few specks of rose here and there; it was common for the tail to be the last part of a dragon to fully catch up to maturity. Now the glorious colour that swept her face and belly and wings had quite taken over her tail, with reds and pinks dancing up and down in vivid illustration. Only a few spots here and there, and the tips of Quartz's wings, remained monochrome.

She spun slowly on the spot and then collapsed in an ungainly heap beside her burgeoning hoard: a far greater heap of shiny things than it had been a week ago, when we first assisted her in carrying her treasures from where she had piled them in the river.

"Does this normally happen so fast?" I asked, my attention still on her rose-and-ruby tail.

"Sometimes," said Quartz, her face colouring to a darker red. "When a newly hoarding dragon spends time with a suitable partner for bonding, it can go faster than usual."

I gave her a warm and reassuring look. "It's Tatiana, of course."

"I'm sure our families won't approve," Quartz said hesitantly.

"Your families love you both," I said firmly. "Your mama will have to learn that this is one match she can't control. As for Mr Rackham, I think he will be relieved to have assistance in chaperoning Tatiana through her first Season. She might have a dragon, but she still needs a husband."

"Yes." Quartz drooped her head a little. "I wish I'd been at her side last summer."

"You know about Mr Fairbanks?"

"Tatiana told me today." The dragon's eyes blazed fiercely. "I'd like to burn that rogue's face off."

"Please form an orderly queue," I retorted. "Not that I'm not delighted for you, Quartz, but why am I here in the middle of the night?"

"Oh." The dragon gave an odd huff, like a giggle. "Wyrmhole magic. I wasn't expecting mine to come in for at least another decade. Mama was forty when hers came upon her!"

"Wyrmhole." I glanced behind me as if that strange passageway into my room was about to rip open again. "This is normal for dragons?" I had heard tales of wyrmholes, but somehow I imagined the process involved actual digging of tunnels, not connecting two unrelated locations and wriggling through.

"How else do you think we collect so many jewels for our hoards?"

"Quartz!" I was quite shocked. "You can't keep stealing from bedrooms!"

She laughed properly at me now, snorting steam out of both nostrils. "No! Not after the first scavenging. Haven't you ever heard of caving?"

"Of course. That's when you go into the mountains and…" To be honest, I'd never thought more about this. "Snuffle about in old jewel mines and such, yes?"

Quartz rolled her enormous gold eyes at me. "It's not like digging for truffles. Once our magic comes in, we can travel inside mountains via wyrmhole, find veins of gold and precious stones that no human could ever reach with their axes and gunpowder. We're not even limited to mountains in our own world. There are lands rich with gold and jewels where no human has ever set foot."

My breath stilled. "You're going to dive off to some other world without telling anyone?"

"I'm telling you, Dimity," said Quartz gently. As if I were the unreasonable one. "I promised Mr Rackham that if I came into my magic, I'd inform someone from the household so you can guard my hoard while I'm gone. Tatiana's not of age yet. And I rather thought Mrs Harefield and Mrs Wrexham might shout at me..."

"Perhaps I'm going to shout at you," I said tartly, and then hugged her with as much of my tiny arms as I could manage. "Don't be gone too long, darling."

"Oh, I'll be back by breakfast!" Quartz said, shimmying so that all her scales gleamed in the lantern light. "Who would miss steak and eggs? I just want to see if I can do it, that's all!"

She shimmied again, with extra wiggle. Before I could say: "Pardon me, Miss de Bramble, did you mean right now, at this very moment?" Quartz had leaped into the air, which ripped open to receive her. She slithered her body through the hole and was gone.

The air mended around her. Watching it happen again made the whole process no less bewildering.

I WAITED in the cottage for over an hour, guarding Quartz's hoard. I could not go back to the house on my own, not without knowing what had happened to her. Besides: no one would be awake yet. I might not be able to find a door unlatched.

Without even a sustaining cup of tea, I curled up on the floor cushions near the hoard, tucking my bare feet up off the cool flagstones, and thought about what I might say to Tatiana if morning came, and Quartz was still gone.

I DID NOT MEAN to sleep, and yet I was jolted awake by the sound of stone striking stone. As I jolted upright, I saw the young dragon standing before me, exhausted and proud of herself, as uncut sapphires rained from the ceiling down on to her hoard.

"Breakfast," she muttered and collapsed happily on the flagstones, her eyes fluttering with exhaustion.

"You'd better sleep," I said, patting her head. "I'll have breakfast brought to you, my dear. You might not be a married lady, but I can't think of anyone more deserving of food on a tray."

It was getting light as I returned to the big house: the back door was ajar, so at least some of the household were awake. I made my way past the kitchens quietly, determined to change into respectable day clothes before I asked the cook to change the usual breakfast arrangements; Quartz likely wouldn't have the energy to chew steak for at least a few hours.

I hurried up the stairs, making for my room. There was an odd smell on the landing, a sort of roses-and-something perfume. Surely no one would be cleaning anything this early; the first hours of the day were for the lighting of fires and making of breakfasts.

Sure enough, one of the housemaids was already in my room when I slipped inside, kneeling on the grate to light my fire. I twitched a robe from its hook in an instant, wrapped it around my nightgown, and then turned to greet her. I would need some sort of excuse as to why I had been out of bed when she arrived...

But no, I would not. The maid did not return my greeting, and when I peered closer, I saw that she was, while kneeling upright, quite asleep. Breathing, but...

The rose smell was stronger, somehow.

I ran to the window and flung it open, then returned to the landing. The room that Dido usually shared with Mr Harefield (when he was not on rescue missions) was on the other side of the staircase, and I made for it, flinging the door open.

It was hardly a surprise that Dido was asleep at this hour, even with me stampeding into her room and flinging open her windows (so much flinging!) to let out the strange rose scent. But when I went to my sister and shook her hard enough for her mob cap to fall off her head, she still did not awaken.

CHAPTER 21
A DARING RESCUE

Dido and Mr Harefield were housed in one of the largest guest suites: designed in the classical style, with a fresco featuring Lady de Bramble's famous mother Corneliar in the guise of an Ancient Empress, facing off against the wicked foreign tyrant Kleopahtrar in a duel of flames and blood.

Most of the bedrooms at Malachite were perfectly modest in dress and style, but a few had fallen prey to Lady B's own preferences in interior design. The fresco was, I believe, a commission she had presented to Mr Rackham upon his twenty-first birthday.

It was a grand room, with windows facing the back of the house. As I ran to those windows to loosen more latches and air out the room, I had a clear view of Carnelians Cottage... and three shadowy figures holding lanterns, bearing down upon Quartz's safe retreat. Upon her new hoard.

My sister, caught in this strange rose-scented sleeping

enchantment, slumbered on. Fresh air was not enough to break the spell.

There was a scream from somewhere in the house above me; so, I was *not* the only one awake. I tore out of Dido's room and up the stairs to the family quarters, heading for Tatiana's bedroom.

The girl was sitting straight up in bed, eyes wide and wild. "Dimity," she choked as I burst through her door. "Quartz is in danger."

"Hunters," I breathed.

A family of hunters had lured away Mr Rackham and Chambrey and Mr Harefield. Someone had cast some manner of sleeping spell on the remainder of the household.

Thanks to our grand tour of the villages, there was no one in the shire who could not be aware that Malachite had a brand-new dragon as a guest; one who was building her hoard, only just coming into her powers...

It wasn't much of a hoard yet, hardly worth stealing. But not all hunters are respectful enough to wait until their prey is fully grown...

And there are many profitable uses for a young, malleable dragon, if you are wicked enough to capture one.

"We're on our own," I told Tatiana. "You and me. We're the only ones left to defend her."

I had never seen the younger girl look fiercer. For a moment, I could have sworn her eyes flashed gold, like a dragon. "Let them just *try* and take her from me."

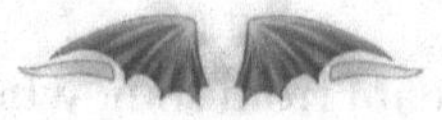

IT WAS foolhardy for two young ladies of a respectable nature to run across the back lawn barefoot, in pursuit of three mysterious cloaked figures. But our dragon was in danger, and there was no one awake to aid us.

We had the foresight to duck into the kitchen on our way through, and we were now both armed with a sturdy copper pan in each hand.

An awful noise came from inside the cottage: a growling scream that could only emanate from the throat of a dragon. Tatiana yelped as if someone had punched her in the ribs. She scrambled ahead of me, into the inner sanctum.

Quartz was screaming. Her scaled body writhed wildly under the glowing pink tangle of a net pricked with tiny pearl beading. A cruel weapon: hunting nets were outlawed a generation ago. The beads were charmed to refract a dragon's magic; to strip her of her power and her connexion to her hoard.

Under the net, Quartz was in pain.

Tatiana was a Fury unleashed. She ran up to the nearest cloaked figure and boxed their ears with both of her copper pans.

There was a short scream, and the creature fell to the ground. A pale face and dark beribboned curls of hair spilled out of the cloak, revealing her identity.

I stared down at the child-like face of little Lavinia Bellamy, heart-shaped mouth and all. She really was too young to be Out.

"Aren't you supposed to be eloping with Gideon Fairbanks?" I demanded.

One of the other cloaked figures made a half-hearted lunge at me, but I smacked her in the stomach with my copper pan and she burst into tears; I barely recognised this one, but I vaguely remembered that her name was Lottie; the second youngest.

The third girl stood over Quartz's writhing body, muttering over what I quickly recognised as a sacred sage-knife. This one was the sorceress. The scent of roses was heavy on her cloak.

"Stop that now," I ordered her.

Lettuce Bellamy (why had I memorised all their names, was there not something more useful I could have learned instead, like Latin or historical facts about queens?) tossed back her own hood. She wore spectacles and was rather more awkward than her pretty sisters, probably because she had spent much of her childhood swotting over magical tomes instead of indulging in fresh air and conversation with friends. In another decade she'd have quite the squint and the familiar stoop of a person with a rich internal life. "You can't stop us," she said scornfully. "Our father is the greatest dragon hunter of a generation."

I snorted. "Fifteen kills are a stain on his character but hardly worthy of the history books. Besides, hasn't he retired?"

"This dragon is ours," said Lettuce, waving her knife again. "You hoarders always want to keep your privileges to yourself. We earned her."

Quartz let out another cry of pain.

"You haven't even successfully abducted her," I said crossly. "We stopped you."

"You can't stop…"

I dropped both copper pans to the flagstones, stepped on the girl's foot, and slapped her in the face.

She stared at me, too shocked to react. "I have a knife."

I kicked her in the knee.

"Ow!"

"Take your net off our dragon right now," I commanded her, summoning my own inner dragon. (When in doubt, *be* Lady Beautrice de Bramble.)

"Shan't!" said Lettuce.

Honestly, how had this girl survived as a middle sibling? Surely the elder two *and* the younger two had tormented her enough to make her immune to such tricks as, for instance, having her hair pulled so hard that her eyes watered?

(When I was seventeen I did that twice a week to Dido by accident, let alone on purpose.)

Lettuce was so startled at having my hand yank her hair that she swung her magical knife around in my direction, catching the side of my face with it.

"Ow!"

Blood ran down my cheek. I wasn't sure who was more surprised; me or the sorceress.

The answer, of course, was the knife itself: one can't go around bloodying a sacred sage-knife and expect it to continue to do your bidding.

Lettuce screamed as pink flames licked up the blade to her hand. She dropped the knife directly on to Quartz.

Our dragon screamed again. The net caught fire, burning pink and gold and then falling apart in ash and smoke.

"That's not fair!" Lettuce wailed petulantly.

I slapped her in the face again, as she clearly deserved it. Then I backed up to the nearest wall and, with some effort, dragged an heirloom sword off its fixings.

A mistake: the thing was so heavy that I could barely keep the hilt upright, let alone the blade, which dragged on the flagstones.

The air around us shivered and groaned. One entire wall of Carnelians Cottage tore away to reveal the mighty shape of a glowing red dragon in her prime. "What is the meaning of this?" roared the real Lady Beautrice de Bramble, storming through the wyrmhole, which sealed instantly behind her.

Now the sanctum was half-filled with dragon: Lady B's enormous, scaled body stood in battle-mode, stretching her webbed wings wide to show off their breadth. It was such an extraordinary entrance that I only belatedly recognised the shaking figure of Leda Bellamy, clinging to the back of the most intimidating dragon of the current era.

Her sisters noticed.

"You traitor!" screamed little Lavinia. I dropped the

heavy sword and stamped on her hand. (It was *right there* and simply begging for such attention. I only wished I was wearing shoes.)

"How could you, Leda?" demanded Lottie, still sobbing and, occasionally, sneezing.

"Mama's going to disown you!" cried Lettuce from where she sat on the floor, cradling her burnt fingers against her chest.

For a moment, Leda looked upset, and then she sat straight-backed on her seat astride the mighty dragon. "You are all a disgrace," she scolded her sisters, in what might well be the first sharp tone she had ever employed on anyone. "You are the three most disagreeable hoydens in existence, and I am embarrassed to know you."

"Indeed," snorted Lady Beautrice. "I've never seen such incompetence in hunters. Don't your people train youngsters properly anymore?" She leaned over Quartz, breathing steam gently over her daughter's scales. "Don't worry, my dear. You may consider yourself thoroughly rescued."

Leda climbed down off the back of the dragon and was immediately accosted by her flailing, accusing sisters. Tatiana ran to Quartz, ducking a wing to reach her without being steamed by Lady B's motherly embrace.

I felt dizzy. The immediate danger was over. Surely I could get some fresh air for a minute. The smell of smoke and roses was still rather...

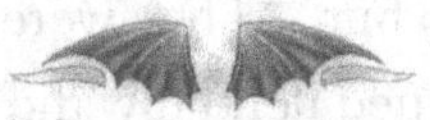

OUTSIDE, I could breathe. I heard was the sound of horses and carriages approaching... many of them, at great speed. Lanterns and shouting.

"Dimity!" called a voice that I recognised as my brother.

I sucked in some more fresh air, distressed beyond all reason that they were going to ask for explanations and oh, *Dido*. Dido was still cursed or something terrible upstairs.

Roses and smoke, and...

"Dimity," said another voice, deep and concerned. Mr Rackham stood right in front of me. Had he travelled by wyrmhole, or merely taken some very long strides? "Dimity, are you..."

"It's all right," I said faintly. "Tatiana and Quartz are perfectly well."

He took a step further into my personal space, looking ever so disgruntled. "I was asking about..."

For a moment, something bright flared between us: I jumped back and away from him, certain that one of Quartz's wyrmholes had, for a brief second, flared into life.

Mr Rackham's eyes would not leave me alone. "Dimity..."

"Ford!" Tatiana came racing out of the cottage like a

fresh foal on unsteady legs. She flung herself at her brother and clung to him. "They were going to take Quartz, and we rescued her. How did you know to return so quickly?"

Rackham kissed the top of his sister's head. "You were very brave," he assured her. "We turned around as soon as we learned we had been tricked."

I noticed a certain sulky lady standing near one of the carriages, shooting resentful glances in my direction.

"Did Miss Laura confess?" I asked, still unsteady on my feet. Dido, we were forgetting Dido...

"No," said Rackham with a twist of his mouth. "But the Bellamy family didn't bribe Fairbanks nearly enough to go along with their plot. He thought spilling their secrets to me might prove more profitable. Never thought I'd be so pleased to have that devil wheedling money off me."

A GREAT MANY things happened over the next few hours.

Dido and the rest of the household were awoken from their enchanted slumber; the rose-scented curse set by Miss Lettuce Bellamy had already begun to dissipate when the sacred sage-knife was destroyed. A physician was called, who pronounced that no one was likely to die of rose inhalation, and really this could have waited until a more civilised hour of the day.

Human and dragon representatives of the Crown, alerted by Lady Beautrice, arrived by air to view the scene and take notes on what had occurred; unlicensed hunting was always taken seriously by the authorities, and crimes against dragons were especially political in the current climate.

A Mr Gracechurch arrived, being the nearest adult relative to the young Bellamy ladies. He brought with him the paperwork necessary (stamped by government officials in triplicate) to take four of his nieces into custody until the Crown determined what was to be done with them.

Miss Leda Bellamy was almost taken along with her sisters, but Lady Beautrice stepped in and declared that she would personally escort the young lady to stay with her local curate and his wife until the family scandal died down.

Chambrey Iverwold kept darting looks of admiration at Miss Bellamy, and commenting loudly on how commendable her bravery was, especially when our sister Dido was glancing in his general direction.

I was aware of all these things, and yet I could not quite feel a proper reaction to any of them.

At one point I slipped away from all the humans and their chatter, making for the cottage. Quartz was still inside, and I had watched Tatiana sneak back in about ten minutes earlier.

I found them together, of course. Quartz had shifted

just enough to rest upon her hoard, her gleaming scales stretched over the shallow heap of sapphires and pennies and other treasures. I could see my strand of pearls tangled gently around one of her claws. Her eyes were closed, and she huffed a little to herself as she napped, steam emerging from her nostrils.

Tatiana leaned against the hoard, her cheek pressing into one of Quartz's red wings as if it was a velvet cushion. Unlike the sleeping dragon, she cracked an eye open when she heard me approach. "They don't need us yet, do they?" she murmured.

"They're all terribly busy," I said, finding an actual cushion to press between me and the cold flagstones, because I had little confidence in dragonflesh to keep me comfortable. "I'm sure they'll remember our existence soon enough."

"I wanted to claw their eyes out," she mumbled. "All those horrid girls. Not very ladylike of me."

"I know for a fact you have a portrait of your Great-Aunt Corneliar leading the army of dragon maids in the Wyvthanian Revolution on your bedroom wall," I replied. "It was your sixth birthday present from your Aunt Beautrice. I don't know how your family could have expected you to grow up entirely demure."

Tatiana let out a small, sleepy giggle.

Quartz huffed half a snore.

My head swam and for a moment I saw it again — a roughly-hewn tear in the air between us, glowing brightly golden. Wyrmhole. I blinked, and it was gone. What was happening to me?

Tatiana let out a low cry, turning towards Quartz. "Oh, no!"

I half-rose, light-headed. I could not quite manage to get to my feet. Together, we watched helplessly as the colour bled out of Quartz's wings and tail and scales, leaving nothing but grey, grey... not even the warm, living greys of a kit not yet showing her mature colours. Before our eyes, this young and vibrant dragon turned to cold, grey stone.

Hibernation.

The deepest sleep.

Gone, beyond our reach.

CHAPTER 22
IN VAIN I HAVE STRUGGLED

I have never known a more wretched summer than those next few weeks at Malachite. The sudden and shocking hibernation of Quartz left everything else drained of colour.

I could not care about the Crown's treatment of the Bellamy sisters, or whether or not Chambrey was now writing secret letters to the one Miss Bellamy who had proven herself a true hero.

I could not even care that Mr Rackham was now, quite certainly, guaranteed to never marry Miss Laura.

(It is possible that I cared a little about that.)

I spent most of my day worried about Tatiana, who had become almost as grave and quiet as the Quartz-shaped statue in Carnelians Cottage. Everyone was worried about Tatiana.

(It is possible that most of the household were equally worried about me.)

"Miss Iverwold," said an exasperated voice above me. I startled awake, from my nest of cushions beside Quartz and her hoard. "This will not do," said Mr Rackham.

I sat up quickly, adjusting my gown. "I don't like to leave her alone. And you will insist on Tatiana having lessons at eleven o'clock every morning."

It was up to the humans who loved Quartz to keep her company, as Lady Beautrice had been driven to such a fury about her daughter's unscheduled hibernation that she had taken to the skies, flying angry laps of Whistwipshire for days at a time.

"I insist," said Mr Rackham gravely. "Because otherwise my sister would spend every hour of the summer imprisoned in this damned cottage."

I gave him a rather wan smile. "Luckily, you do not have the same authority over me as your sister, Mr Rackham."

He honoured me with a disapproving expression. I had received many of these over the last several weeks; this was a particularly fine example of the species. "Miss Iverwold. It has been four weeks. You must accept..."

I had heard this speech before. I got to my feet, patting my hair and looking around for where I had discarded my bonnet. "I need accept nothing that I deem unacceptable, Mr Rackham, and whatever is about to come out of your mouth is likely..."

"If she has not woken yet," he said in decisive tones. "It becomes more likely that she will sleep through the winter."

"No," I snapped back with the same ferocity I had summoned last time he suggested such a thing.

There were two weeks of summer left. I had cancelled all of my stays elsewhere, refusing to leave Malachite and Tatiana and Quartz. Dido had quietly cancelled many of her own previous commitments, making it seem as if we had always intended to remain this long as guests of the Rackham family.

"Dimity," Rackham sighed.

"No," I said, letting him see a little of the fury and frustration I had been concealing for weeks. "Dragons *never* begin their hibernation in summer. If she does not wake soon... it's all wrong. She must wake, or she might never..."

My shoulders shook, but I composed myself after a moment. It would not do to lose my dignity, not in front of the most dignified man in the world.

Summer is for hunting, autumn is for hoarding, so the tales say. Quartz should be here in autumn, fossicking for pebbles in the river and darting in and out of abandoned diamond mines via wyrmhole.

Rackham gave a deep sigh, recognising that he had pressed too hard, and that (once again) nothing would come of it. There was no stubbornness to match mine.

"Dimity," he said in a gentler tone. "Would you care

to take a walk with me? I have stationed three footmen outside the cottage. Quartz will be safe if you leave her for a little while."

"But lonely," I murmured.

"I shouldn't worry about that," said a voice at the doorway. A footman entered, carrying a straight-backed chair, followed by my sister Dido. "I have a great deal of knitting to do," she said, waving her yarn bag at me. "So many babies due in the next few months! I may as well knit bonnets and bootlings in here as anywhere."

No more excuses. Fresh air it was.

READER, I went for a walk. The afternoon sunshine was perfectly excellent, but I felt little of the warmth upon my face. My thoughts were with Quartz, cold as stone.

It was clear that Mr Rackham wished to speak to me of something significant. I caught him fidgeting with his handkerchief more than once, which was far from his usual manner.

"Leaving aside the circumstances of your extended stay," he began. "It has been most..."

"Do you wish us to leave?" I interrupted.

He gave me an expression I could only interpret as fond exasperation. "Not in the least. We wouldn't wish to give Iverwold any ideas about returning to Elderflower Hall, after all."

This was intended as a joke, I suppose, but I had no spirit to pretend I found anything amusing.

"Perhaps we should have stayed there," I said grimly. "Then none of this would have come to pass."

Mr Rackham blinked. "Dimity, surely you cannot blame yourself for what has occurred? You were not even at Carnelians when Miss Laura saw Quartz for the first time and recognised her budding condition."

That was true enough. Still, my sour thoughts struggled to see reason.

I made no response to his statement. There was little point in discussing my guilt if he was so eager to deny me that comfort.

After walking in silence for a while, Rackham began to speak again. "I know that the timing is not... and yet when has there ever been... I am a fool to not have asked you at the beginning of the summer, but there have been so many distractions for us both..."

I stopped. He appeared to have lost all ability to form a complete sentence, and it was difficult to pay attention to his ramshackle words while also walking. "Mr Rackham, what are you about?"

He gave me a remarkably helpless expression, for a man who has never been the least bit helpless. "In vain I have struggled," he began.

A sizzling sound cut through the gentle morning. A ragged golden tear opened up in the air before us. For a moment I thought it was Quartz, alive and playing with her new magic once more, but there was no familiar face on the other side of this strange wyrmhole, merely a golden fog.

"What the devil is that?" Rackham exclaimed.

"Oh," I said in surprise. "You can see it too."

"Of course I can — Dimity, don't touch it!"

I was already drifting forward, my hand outstretched. I could feel the warmth on my fingertips, brighter than the sun. "I think I must."

He seized hold of my waist in both hands, like he was lifting me in the midst of a country dance. "Dimity."

My mind was clouding over. Why did he sound so afraid? Warmth was comfort. Light was home. Heat roared in my ears. I took a step forward, and felt nothingness beneath my feet...

Mr Rackham did not let go of my waist. I have no doubt he was shouting some intelligent advice, but I was beyond the realm of hearing anything he had to say.

The ground came up to meet us both and we fell, rolling on to a lawn made of grass as sparkling gold as any tiara.

I lay on my back, gasping for air, staring at clouds in a sky that was entirely the wrong colour.

"Dimity," groaned Mr Rackham beside me. "What have you done?"

I sat up, staring around at the strange new land in which we had found ourselves. "Mr Rackham," I said. "Please do not be alarmed, but I believe I may be turning into a dragon."

He let out a sound that could only be described as

utter frustration, writ large. "Yes," he said finally, in leaden tones. "That's about where I saw this day going."

CHAPTER 23

WHERE DRAGONS SLEEP

The sky was silver, the grass was gold. The nearest trees were black silhouettes dripping with ruby fruit. We were no longer in Malachite.

Mr Rackham took it rather well, all things considered. I was in rather more of a, shall we say, delicate state.

The strange and alarming beauty of the landscape curling around us was barely of interest to me, not when I saw the sparkling pond. I hurried towards it with a dedicated fervour, throwing myself at its edge despite the risk to my best muslin (which had suffered indignities enough thanks to being slept in all night during my vigil in Carnelians Cottage).

"Dimity," said the concerned voice of Mr Rackham behind me. "Are you quite well?"

I stared at my face in the reflection. It appeared the same as usual, perhaps a little paler, made plain by exhaustion and sadness. I did not have scales.

"What are you looking for?" I heard behind me as he approached, speaking in a measured tone as if trying not to spook me.

"Change," I replied. "Is there more gold in my hair than usual? The sunshine is so bright, I cannot be certain."

There was a long pause, and when he spoke it was with an air of concern. "You do not truly believe you are transforming into a dragon?"

I waved my arms, not wishing to look at him. Perhaps he might spot a gleam of sapphire in my irises, though there was little sign of it in my reflection. "How else did this happen? I have been seeing visions of wyrmholes since Quartz was taken from us. Something bewildering is happening to me."

"But not that." His hand, careful as always, slid under my elbow to help me up. I went as I always did, following his lead. Trusting. "Dimity. There is a much simpler explanation for this preposterous scenario in which we find ourselves."

"And what is that?" I stared at his chest, not ready to look at his face. Mr Rackham was always so tidy, even when flung into unreal magical realms.

He touched a fingertip to my chin, and now I did look up, into his face. His calming, reassuring, familiar face. "Someone brought us here," Rackham said quietly. "We will know more when we understand who, and why."

He glanced up, as shadows danced through the fluffy clouds in the silver sky above us. Dragons in flight. We were not the only creatures alive in this glittering land.

We might, however, be the only humans.

We might indeed, I realised later, be the only humans who had *ever* set foot in this land. By now we had crested a hillside or two, examined a little wilderness (not quite a forest) and determined that there were no man-made structures in evidence.

There was a road, wide and flat and curling: the kind made by hundreds of years of clawed feet treading the same route. There was no evidence of cobblestones or flagstones, carriage houses or stables, or any other marks of human civilisation and transportation...

Why would one need any of those things, when wings and wyrmholes were available?

"We should speak to someone," said Rackham, still attempting to sound in control of the situation, though we were both so thoroughly ungrounded from familiar territory. "Perhaps the dragons of this land have a spokesperson..."

If they were society dragons, that was a reasonable assumption. But what if they were wild? I had never in my life had any reason to be afraid of a dragon, but that was when one could fall back upon the manners and mores of our world.

What were we to do if the philosophy in this land of silver skies was to roast first and ask questions later?

A shape darkened the sun above us. A large, wide shadow descended. Mr Rackham neatly drew me under the branches of a tree, which shivered with pearl-encrusted fruit. As the dragon landed on the golden grass, several of those fruits fell as if the mighty wing-flaps had caused a vibration all the way up into the branches and twigs.

A large clump of pearl-and-silver dropped into my bosom; I twitched it out and tossed it aside before Mr Rackham caught me in such an undignified moment.

The dragon that faced us had long blue whiskers protruding from either side of his snoot, and eyes that shone like the brightest, most valuable jewels. He was perhaps three-quarters the size of Lady Beautrice, but no less terrifying. Steam gushed from his nostrils, mouth and ears as if he was working up a good flame with which to grill us.

"Humans have no place here," he declared in a voice that was half-roar, half-rumble. "What is your reason for this trespass?"

Mr Rackham, trained in the art of dragon diplomacy and society manners from a very young age, bowed smartly at the waist. "My lord," he began, as a matter of standard discourse with an unknown patron. "May I..."

"Peg," I squeaked from where I stood behind him.

"What," said Mr Rackham.

I peeked again. The mighty dragon's eyes brightened with a greater ferocity. "Lord Peregrine," I corrected myself, though indeed this dragon had once told me that I was to call him Peg, as that was how his friends addressed him. "We met several years ago, at my coming out ball. I'm Dimity Iverwold. Mrs Harefield's sister."

Mr Rackham and I both held our breath. At least, I trust he was doing so. It was the only sensible action under the circumstances.

Lord Peregrine's eyelids batted twice, with an audible creak. He opened his jaws as if about to incinerate us both with a mighty breath...

"Why, Miss Iverwold," he growled. "Of course, I recall such a charming young lady."

I hurtled ahead, since manners were doing the trick, and nobody had yet died. "May I introduce Mr Rackham, a dear family friend? Mr Rackham, this is Lord Peregrine Annesley, patron to the Terminster-Bollivar families." A dragon, I now recalled, who had not awoken from hibernation for two years.

Rackham nodded his head stiffly. "I know of you, sir, indeed, though we have not before been introduced. I'm sure you are acquainted with my..."

Thoughts were racing through my head. The jewelled trees and strange sky. The wild dragons.

"Is this where you come when you sleep in stone?" I blurted out.

Both gentlemen, dragon and human alike, stared at me. Had I said something terribly rude? It was such a strange day, it was hard to remember what was appropriate.

"This land," growled Lord Peregrine "call-me-Peg" with rather less charm than he had exhibited on the dance floor, "Is a secret reserved for dragons. You should not be here."

"I agree, sir," said Mr Rackham. "And yet, we have been brought here against our will."

"It was such a surprise," I agreed.

Another shadow flickered over our heads. Lord Peregrine threw back his neck and let out an uncouth reptilian cry, such as one would never hear in the streets or assembly halls of Abberline.

A new dragon landed on the golden grass, this one head and shoulders above Lord Peregrine. His scales were a dappled amethyst with flecks of red here and there. I had seen him from afar at some of the grandest society balls, but not for years, not since...

"Lord Belvedere," breathed Rackham, bowing even deeper than he had for Lord Peregrine. Lord Belvedere, who had been patron to the Queen herself a decade ago. I recalled that he was neatly replaced by his granddaughter shortly after one long winter hibernation sent flutters of worry through the palace.

Jewel-purple eyes flashed. "Why, it's young Fordyce Rackham, nephew to Lady Beautrice de Bramble," snarled the newcomer, flexing his muscles and swishing a tail as thick as a tree trunk.

"Your aunt's not here, is she?" put in Lord Peregrine, looking alarmed.

"My aunt believes hibernation to be a waste of everyone's time," said Mr Rackham, with a wry twist of his mouth. "She prefers to hibernate as briefly as possible in the middle of winter and would happily eschew the privilege if she could keep her eyes open all year around."

"Aren't we thankful for that," Lord Peregrine muttered, amused with himself.

"What is this incursion?" demanded Lord Belvedere the Elder. "Humans in our land? Did your aunt send you?"

Even a world ruled by dragons had something to fear and it was, apparently, Lady Beautrice de Bramble.

"Not at all," Mr Rackham answered immediately, then paused to consider. "At least, she did not tell me this was her intention. I do not know who is responsible for our transport here."

"We are looking for Miss Quartz de Bramble," I put in. "Lady Beautrice's young daughter." If this was where sleeping dragons came when they turned to stone, then we must find her here. Must we not?

"Ahhhhh," said Lord Belvedere thoughtfully, raking his claws on the grass. "Finally, the matter resolves into an *answer*."

I was glad somebody thought so.

"If it were possible to direct me to my cousin," Mr Rackham said, in a manner I could only describe as valiant. "We do not wish to inconvenience you with our presence."

Red sparks flashed in the jewel-purple eyes of Lord Belvedere. "As our friend here is hardly of a size to transport two humans..." he began in a rumble.

"Oh, I say," protested Lord Peregrine.

"...I shall have to partake of that honour," the larger dragon concluded.

My hand reached out. Somehow, Mr Rackham found it without further ado, wrapping his strong hand around mine. It was not nearly enough comfort. Would I shock the dragons if I demanded he put his arms entirely around me?

"The honour is ours, my lord," said Mr Rackham.

I could not think of a single thing to say.

Dragonback. I had not even ridden upon Quartz's back let alone a dragon of Lord Belvedere's size. *And* we had not even been introduced!

Adventures would be so much more pleasant if one were adequately warned ahead of time as to what particular excitements were to be experienced. Like a menu on a tea table.

Dragonback was not something one should attempt without having properly prepared oneself!

(And yet, how could one prepare oneself for something so extraordinary? I would never know. When it happened to me, it was with barely a minute's notice.)

Luckily, something else entirely extraordinary happened immediately before the exercise, which proved a pleasant distraction from the terrifying prospect of taking flight.

As Lord Belvedere knelt to receive Mr Rackham and myself upon his wide and scaly back, he stared directly at me and demanded: "Who is this, Young Fordyce? Your young lady?"

I opened my mouth to explain that I was in fact a mere family friend, when Mr Rackham said something which quite knocked me for six.

He said: "yes."

CHAPTER 24
THE RULES OF SLEEPING DRAGONS

Any sensible young lady will spend a reasonable amount of time considering her future. How are you to make sensible decisions about said future if you have not already considered all possible paths of possibility?

Never in my life had I imagined that riding dragonback might be something expected of me, at any time of life.

Aside from the occasional emergency or life-saving endeavour, any member of society in good standing may rub shoulders with dozens or even hundreds of dragons without being called upon to sit atop one and cling on for dear life with one's *knees*.

Dragons are simply not designed to be ridden. They wear no saddles or reins like horses, and thus there is nothing reassuringly solid to grasp. I, who had only before ridden side-saddle (and that imperfectly, sporadically, with little enthusiasm) found it a particular trial to balance with hundreds of pounds of pulsating reptilian skin and bone and flesh beneath me. My crumpled muslin day dress needed to be ripped up one side so that I could spread my thighs wide enough to be remotely safe, and my fingers were wound so tightly into the thin, leathery webbing of Lord Belvedere's purple wings that I was sure one or both of us would end up bleeding.

Indignity upon indignity.

Added to that the whooshing pressure of the air as we flew along the tops of the trees, the yawning fear of falling, the unbearable chill whipping against my arms despite the amiable sunshine beating down upon us.

All this, and I was likely to end up with a sun-burn, as my bonnet had flown away when we first left the ground.

Added to that, *Mr Rackham, Mr Rackham, Mr Rackham.*

The gentleman in question sat behind me, by necessity far closer than ever would be deemed appropriate. His thighs brushed the backs of my legs, and his chest was a streak of heat along my back. He had twisted one hand into the web of Mr Belvedere's wings to steady himself, and the other hand remained resolutely upon my waist.

We had a great deal to discuss. I could only hope to manage conversation at this height without hurling the contents of my last meal into the winds around us.

Bronze-and-topaz trees gleamed below, like we were flying over the contents of a jeweller's tray writ large upon the landscape.

"Mr Rackham," I said, my throat dry with cold air

and travel dust. "What did you mean when you spoke thus to our host?"

"*Is this your young lady?*"

"*Yes.*"

There was only one thing he could have meant by that, unless he was deliberately speaking an untruth, and one did not lie to dragons if one wished to keep all of one's limbs.

"You know what I meant," Mr Rackham replied, his mouth so close to my ear that it felt entirely improper. "Dimity, I know that my proposal was interrupted, but surely the intent was…"

"*Proposal?*"

"Yes."

"When?"

"In the lane, shortly before…"

"I know it has been a trying day, and I have been rather distracted, but surely I would have noticed if you…"

"I was working up to it!" He sounded rather irritated, but there was no time for coddling his feelings on the matter. I was so thoroughly astonished that it was a miracle I had not slid off this undulating dragon and landed in a tree.

There is something about flying dragonback that renders one short of breath and also of reason. My mind was flying faster than the dragon.

"When?" I asked again, more sharply than before.

"I told you, in the lane…"

"No. *Since* when have you wished to marry me?" I would not allow myself to get carried away by thoughts of future happiness if I was to be a consolation prize after the disaster that was Laura Bellamy.

"I asked my aunt for the family ring at the end of this Season of Dragons," said Mr Rackham.

"For *me?*" Tatiana and Quartz had certainly not thought so.

"Dimity," he said, leaning (if possible) even closer, so that his voice was rough in my ear. "I never considered giving it to another."

"But Miss Laura…" who rejected a proposal at the rectory that Rackham claimed he never intended to offer…

He growled into the back of my neck. This produced a rather more pleasing sensation than one might imagine. "I would be a happy man to never hear the name of Bellamy ever again."

"You admired her fine eyes," I said in a small voice. "You said they were brightened by the exercise." On the day that Laura Bellamy arrived with mud on her hem, demanding to visit her ailing sister.

"Dimity," sighed Rackham. "You had just bounded down several flights of stairs and practically thrown your-self into my arms. I was talking about *your* eyes. I was always talking about your eyes."

"You said it was pleasant when a lady did not hesitate to speak her mind."

"How is it you have memorised a list of former

compliments and yet you never guessed their intended target?"

My thoughts were like a jumbled mass of embroidery threads, tied in knots and impossible to unravel. "We have known each other for *years*."

I had been Out for years. Perfectly available for marriage for years... should someone deign to ask. Unless there was some reason he had held back — disapproval from his aunt? Waiting for our Countess to wake up and make me a better prospect? What?

Something soft brushed against the back of my neck and I realised with a delightful shiver that it was a kiss. "Your brother told me once that he felt Dido married too young. She was obliged to make a swift match because your father was ailing... She is happy with Mr Harefield, and yet had little time to truly enjoy society before she was made a matron."

"When did my brother say this?" I demanded. Chambrey. What a meddler he was. And how like him to capture the interest of such a suitor by suggesting he refrain from courting me.

"At your Coming Out ball," said Mr Rackham, his hand a little firmer on my waist. "Brace yourself, I think..."

The air, thick in my ears, became a swoosh and a dip as Lord Belvedere brought us down in a clearing, surrounded by metallic trees.

I felt the landing in my bones and could not quite relax my hold on the wings.

Mr Rackham's comforting warmth disappeared from behind me and then he was standing beneath my left hip, hands outstretched to help me down. I lurched to one side, hands brushing his shoulders, and he lifted me as if we were in the middle of a country dance.

For one brief moment, he held me, and I stared into his eyes.

"A rescue mission, I believe," snarled the genteel tones of Lord Belvedere. "If you two have the leisure."

"Dimity!" chimed a familiar voice. "Cousin Rackham!"

We turned, quickly. Mr Rackham's hands still rested on my waist as the gleaming figure of Quartz — so small, in comparison to Lord Belvedere's majesty — bounded towards us.

She looked *well*. Her eyes were bright, her scales gleaming rose-pink and ruby-red, without a single scale of grey to be seen. "How are you here?" she demanded, curious rather than accusatory. "I don't think there have ever been humans here before..."

"There have not," growled Lord Belvedere. "This is a shocking breach of protocol."

"We apologise for the transgression," Mr Rackham said, as smoothly as if he was negotiating with a banker or solicitor. "Unfortunately, we still have no idea who summoned us, but if my cousin requires an escort home..."

Lord Belvedere made a scoffing sound deep in his larynx.

Another voice, cold and proud, broke into our little gathering. "They are here, Lord Belvedere, because I summoned them. Surely you do not consider yourself so high and mighty that you can disapprove of anything I chuse to do?"

A new dragon entered the clearing, larger than Lord Belvedere, with a longer neck and shorter jawline. Even with the sunshine dimmed slightly by the trees overhead, the wyvern's scales were the brightest, gleamingest emerald green, shading all the way to the palest jade on the tips of her wings.

"Countess," I breathed. Faced for the first time in more than twelve years with my esteemed patroness, the Countess of Chambrey, I hadn't the least idea how to react.

Around me, the others bowed and murmured polite greetings. Even Lord Belvedere bowed, though it was as reluctant a bow as I have ever seen outside an assembly hall.

And I — having waited so long for this meeting, so anxious to show my patroness how well I had done all these years, how proud she should be of how I had grown up...

I burst into tears.

CRYING IS A MESSY, tedious business. I do not recommend it.

I SHALL NOT SHARE the intimate or specific details of the conversation that occurred between myself and the Countess, on that strange day, in that strange land. Suffice to say, it was never going to meet all of my expectations after so long and agonising a wait.

Still, I felt satisfied, when we parted. The Countess had received the reports of my father's death, my sister's marriage, and my brother's journey towards reaching his majority without being swindled of his fortune.

She grilled me on the ladylike accomplishments I had acquired over the last fourteen years, paying particular attention to my skills in needlework and the cutting of paper silhouettes, a craft she was quite certain she should have excelled at herself, had she ever learned.

She even listened with what felt like an approving air as I confessed the recent and rather bungled proposal from Mr Rackham. She went on to assure me with a smoky snort that, were the Countess of Chambrey still at large in Abberline society, the son of Old Mr Rackham would have been upon the very short list of gentlemen she considered worthy of her ward.

As our time together grew short, my patroness batted her enormous golden eyes at me and gave me an expression that could only be described as impish. "Never mind all those sensible matters, my dear," said the Countess of Chambrey. "Tell me of everything splendid and strange that occurred during the last Season of Dragons... and the Season before that! You would think we would be up to date with all the best gossip out here, and yet no one ever tells me what I really wish to know! The entertainments. The decorations. The menus."

AFTER OUR CONVERSATION came to a close, the Countess led me back to the patch of trees where Mr Rackham waited with Quartz. Lord Belvedere had long-since flown away, offended at being used as a pack mule and not even receiving a thank you from the Countess.

"You brought us here?" Mr Rackham asked, one hand resting protectively on the back of Quartz's neck.

"I did indeed," said the Countess. "Quite against the rules, but this little one had got herself rather stuck. Hibernation is not for summer," she added sternly to Quartz. "By rights we should make you stay until next Season, when you could wake up on your own. I under-stand you had a shock, little one. But we cannot play fast and loose with the rules, if this land is to remain the haven that it is."

"I don't believe you have ever been constrained by

rules," I blurted. Why could I never keep such thoughts inside my head?

The Countess laughed in a low rumble. I had forgotten her laugh. It was the nicest sound I had heard in a very long while. "To break the rules of sleeping dragons," she said. "One must be at least a Countess, if not a Marquess. And now, it is time to wake up."

CHAPTER 25
HOW TO MARRY A DRAGON

"**O**h," said Quartz, as the fresh wyrmhole cast by the Countess of Chambrey ripped the air open in a sparkle of golden light. Through the hole, we could see the inner sanctum of Carnelians Cottage, with the sleeping dragon statue in the centre of the grey flagstones. "There I am."

"There you are," said the Countess. "Do you remember how to wake up now?"

"I do!" The living, rose-pink Quartz blinked her eyes wildly and then faded from thin air.

Dido, as per her promise to me, was seated in a chair beside the statue, knitting fallen from her hands as she stared at us. Chambrey sat beside her on a second chair, diligently assisting her by winding her wool, as he used to do for our mother when we were very small.

Dido gasped. "Dimity? *Countess?*"

Chambrey scraped his own chair back, lost for words.

Our patroness inclined her jewel-green head. "My

dears," she said. "I'm so very proud of how well you have done without me. I know that I rather left you in the lurch."

Chambrey cleared his throat. "Ah, well," he said airily, showing no sign of the years of hurt in his cheerful tone. "It is the way of things, is it not? Our family were fortunate to have you for so long." He frowned a little. "Rackham, is that you? Gadding about in some sort of magical land with my sister?"

Humour gleamed in the eyes of the Countess. "I can assure you they were properly chaperoned by several respectable dragons."

Yes. Chaperoned the entire time. Every single minute accounted for. I allowed Rackham to hand me through the wyrmhole, hoping very much that there was no stain of blush upon my cheeks.

"You should fetch Tatiana," I told Rackham as he joined the rest of us in the cottage. "Quartz is waking up."

Pink slowly flooded across the still stone of the dragon statue.

Rackham kissed my hand before letting go. He hurried off in search of his sister.

That left the three of us — the children of Emmet Iverwold, grandchildren of Edmund Iverwold — gazing through a golden wyrmhole at our patroness. Former patroness? Dowager patroness?

Dido cleared her throat. "It is good to see you, Countess," she said. "I do not expect you will be coming back this way again?"

The Countess snorted a smoke ring from her elegant

snoot. She was so bright in that other land — brighter than I remember her from childhood. "I was an old lady when I was given the gift of a new family," she declared. "Your family. I had already watched generations die for centuries, before my former family reached the end of their line. There comes a time when there is nothing left of a dragon but fatigue, and aching bones."

"And when you sleep," I murmured. "You are young again."

The Countess grinned her brilliant grin, teeth sharp and visible around the entire line of her jaw. "We miss the assemblies," she confessed. "The balls, the gossip, the saucers of tea. Sometimes it is enough to lure us back, for a season or two. Perhaps I shall do so again someday. Do not wait for me, my dears. You are doing marvellously."

She bowed her green head. The wyrmhole closed.

I no longer felt the need to weep. Perhaps I would not need to again for at least another decade.

AFTER LADY BEAUTRICE DE BRAMBLE checked and double checked that her newly-awoken daughter was well, she turned her attention to me. "I expect you await your reward, Miss Iverwold," she said in tones half-scathing and half-haughty. (I later learned from Rackham that this was a tone generally employed with people she liked.)

"I have no such expectation, Lady Beautrice," I replied in perfect politeness. "I am merely glad to have Quartz back with her family and in such good spirits."

The large dragon arched her neck at me, giving me the kind of baleful eye that might easily wither a lady less content in her happiness than I.

We all sat in the garden parlour, on the ground floor of Malachite. The enormous triple-doors opened into one of the prettier lawns of the estate, and the room was flooded with sunlight which quite cheered the grey stonework.

There were no rugs or antimacassars; this was a room designed for entertaining dragons without creating unnecessary work for the staff.

The chairs were nevertheless comfortable, and the light good enough for Dido to continue her knitting when we gathered as a... shall I say as a family? Mr Rackham had as yet made no announcement about our engagement. Now I came to think of it, I had not yet managed a moment alone with him to inform him of my acceptance. But all things in good time.

Lady Beautrice was in a challenging mood. "Do you mean to say that you will not accept a reward for having rescued my daughter twice, Miss Iverwold? Firstly, from that dreadful little band of upstart hunters, and secondly, from her premature ascent into That Place?"

"Both rescues were shared efforts, Lady Beautrice," I reminded her with a gentle smile.

"And you would have my family remain in debt to you for the sake of pride?"

"Aunt, this really is not a fair line of questioning," broke in Rackham.

Lady Beautrice hissed at him. "Quiet, nephew. This is in your interest."

"I fail to see why it should be to my benefit for you to perform such an interrogation upon my intended."

Dido dropped her knitting.

"Oh, finally, are we allowed to talk about this?" boomed Chambrey from the sideboard, where he had been pouring himself a second whiskey. "Felicitations to you both, may I wish you every happiness, when's the wedding?"

Dido looked genuinely shocked as she pieced together the evidence (it was hardly my fault she had not noticed how close Mr Rackham was sitting to me, and how I could barely keep a silly smile off my face). "Dimity? Is this true?"

"It most certainly is not true," roared Lady Beautrice. "If any member of my family wishes to embark upon marriage, I expect them to gain my blessing!"

Mr Rackham gave her a positively dragonish glare. "I did exactly that, Aunt Beautrice, when I requested the family ring several months ago."

She waved a claw. "You did not say it was for Miss Iverwold."

"I did not need to," he said in deadly tones.

Her eyes glowed with fury. "Did you not?"

"Oh, please do not fight!" requested Tatiana, from where she sat on the hearth-rug, one hand stroking Quartz's back. "Why should there be any argument? If

Aunt B wishes to reward Dimity, it is nothing to be upset about..."

"Indeed," said Dido calmly, returning to her knitting. "Did you have something in mind, Lady Beautrice?"

Lady Beautrice, ready for war, had not expected peace talks to enter the fray quite so quickly. Steam puffed out of her ears. "Any young lady valiant enough to rescue a dragon twice should have the sense to request a boon," she said, rather sullenly. "And if my daughter is to bond with a human, I should like to think I might be consulted."

I glanced around. Everyone else looked just as confused. "Am I to understand that you believe I have bonded with Quartz?"

"Such a match would be impossible without my permission," sniffed Lady Beautrice.

"Then we are in accord," I replied sweetly. "It is indeed impossible."

She snarled at me. "Do you not wish to bond with my daughter? Now that your own dragon has confirmed her neglect of your family to be a permanent arrangement, can you afford to let your pride stand in the way of such a generous offer?"

"Mama," Quartz said cautiously. "As for my bond..."

"Be quiet, daughter," Lady Beautrice said imperiously. "I am negotiating on your behalf. It is entirely appropriate that you bond with the future Mrs Rackham. Honour, decorum and prudence demand it."

"They can demand all they like," I said, remaining polite. My hand slid a little closer to Mr Rackham's leg.

His hand brushed against mine, and then engulfed it entirely. "I am afraid you must be disappointed in this, Lady Beautrice."

If possible, Lady Beautrice's scarlet scales grew even brighter than before. "Obstinate, headstrong girl! Am I to understand you refuse my offer?"

"No legitimate offer has been made, my lady. Only Quartz may chuse her future bondmate, and I am certain that she has not chosen me."

A long silence fell upon the room. Lady Beautrice glared daggers at Quartz, and at Tatiana, who looked the closest to defiant that I had ever seen her. "Is my daughter then to follow this child into some other family of no particular name?" she demanded.

"I have higher aspirations than that, Lady Beautrice," said Miss Tatiana Rackham, her voice rising in confidence. "I fully intend to dedicate myself to spinsterhood. So, you needn't worry. Quartz is not going anywhere."

"I HAVE NEVER BEFORE WITNESSED such determination to be furious about a happy ending," said Mr Rackham, a while later. We had taken advantage of the general drama of Lady Beautrice snapping and snarling her way to Carnelians Cottage for a good sulk, by making a hasty retreat. Now the two of us walked together across the grounds of the Malachite estate.

"Do not worry about your aunt," I assured him, my hand nestled comfortably in the crook of his arm. "She will recover her composure soon enough. By next Season we shall hear her boasting to all that every match made here this summer was entirely her own design."

"You *are* to marry me then?" It was not the first time he had requested confirmation; even after I accepted him, he remained anxious to make up for the insufficiency of his first, interrupted proposal.

"I believe I could be convinced." The Rackham family betrothal ring weighed heavily on my hand; anyone who wished to separate it from me now would have to use an axe.

"You have no quests for me? No impossible tasks so that I may prove my love? No villain to overthrow? I know what kind of books you like to read."

I laughed at him. "I will require you to show me any secret passages in your house after the wedding. And introduce me to any family ghosts."

"Easily done."

"So, there *are* secret passages?" I had never found one in Malachite, though I had been looking for more than a decade!

Rackham gave me an amused sort of glance; I had never seen him so pleased with himself. "Also, ghosts."

I gave a happy sigh. Truly, my future home had everything an eligible gentlewoman might wish. "There may be one quest," I admitted after a moment's thought. "Or perhaps it would be more accurate to call it a scheme.

But it can wait until next Season. That is the only time for matchmaking, after all."

My future husband groaned. "I will not bring Tatiana Out that early," he warned me.

"No, indeed. Let us give her all the time she requires to prepare for a future of dedicated spinsterhood. I was thinking of my brother."

"Iverwold?" Rackham sounded confused. He would learn to keep up with me soon enough.

"I have decided that my plan to protect him from the marriage market was far too risky. Too many variables. The only sensible course is to find him the *right* wife, as efficiently as possible."

Rackham smiled again, catching on to my plan. "No hunters?"

"Of fortunes *or* dragons. I am sure between us, we can find the perfect match."

"I look forward to admiring your schemes from close quarters, Miss Iverwold," said Mr Rackham, with every appearance of sincerity

"You will make an excellent partner in plotting," I assured him. "Once you have completed the requisite training."

We had reached a little wilderness beyond the rose garden which rendered us a moment of complete privacy, where none might observe us from any window in the house (as long as they were not flying overhead at an inopportune moment). Mr Rackham took advantage of this brief interlude to bend down and kiss me, a kiss which I returned with all due appreciation.

"Schemes, plots and matchmaking," said Mr Rack-ham, brushing a stray curl of hair back from my face. "Are you absolutely certain, Miss Iverwold, that you are not a dragon in disguise?"

I sighed with happiness at the mere thought of it. "Oh, my dearest. Wouldn't that be *marvellous*?"

THE END

About the Author

Tansy Rayner Roberts is an award-winning Australian science fiction and fantasy author who prefers crafting to attending parties, and has never wondered if she might be turning into a dragon. She lives with her family in lutruwita/Tasmania.

- Listen to Tansy on Sheep Might Fly, a podcast where she reads aloud her stories as audio serials.
- Read Tansy's stories before anyone else when you pledge to her Patreon.
- What tea is Tansy drinking? Find out when you subscribe to her excellent newsletter: tinyurl.com/tansyrr
- Follow Tansy on Bookbub so you never miss a release.

facebook.com/TansyRRoberts

instagram.com/tansyrr

patreon.com/tansyrr

bookbub.com/authors/tansy-rayner-roberts

AFTERWORD

Thank you for reading this novel! Literally a pet project of mine (if dragons are pets, then a collection of different editions of *Pride and Prejudice* also counts as a pet, right?), this book began in a lightning-strike flutter of sympathy for Caroline Bingley, and wormed (wyrmed) its way under my skin.

I never thought I'd rewrite another classic novel after the epic adventure that was *Musketeer Space*, my gender-swapped space opera chapter-by-chapter retelling of *The Three Musketeers*, but here we are ten years later.

This one is shorter, at least!

I first fell in love with *Pride and Prejudice* thanks to the Greer Garson-Laurence Olivier movie which I acquired somehow on VHS and watched obsessively through my childhood. Then came that Other Amazing Version, you know the one, with Jennifer Ehle and Colin Firth (not to mention the spectacular Anna Chancellor or as we always refer to her in our household, Duckface, playing a particularly vicious Caroline Bingley)*. Then an illustrated edition of the book which I found in my uni bookshop and pored over because it included replicas of the vintage illustrations.

Then... I'm not sure what came next. The obsession has always been there. Somehow. the world's obsession with Jane Austen has grown alongside mine, so that her fame and brand-recognition is somehow greater than it was forty years ago when I first set eyes on Greer Garson and, thanks to the wonders of black and white film, simply assumed Lizzy was a blonde.

Pride and Prejudice is a complex book that contains multitudes. It has a remarkable structure that somehow remains whole even when retold in radically different spaces — such as *Bride and Prejudice*, the first adaptation that made me think it possible that all the Bennet sisters liked each other, or *The Lizzy Bennet Diaries* which took the brilliant angle of retelling most of the marriage plots as career plots, and the bold angle of making Lydia Bennet an incredibly sympathetic character. (Most adaptations don't do this because as soon as you sympathise with Lydia, *P&P* becomes a tragedy instead of a comedy.)

Most recently I was fascinated to read Courtney Milan's brilliant essay in the Michigan Law Review, Pride and Predators, based on the premise that Austen knew exactly what she was doing when she set out to write a book about sexual predators and how social sanc-

---

* Her face is lovely! Blame Richard Curtis and *Four Weddings and a Funeral* for that one.

were the greatest protection we had against such behaviour.

There are always new layers to uncover, and consider, in a book this complex. But at the same time... it's a novel. A jolly good novel. A hell of a read. There's a reason that Austen's work survived her era; not because everyone was in love with her books during her (too-short) lifetime, but because 50 years after her death, her books were reprinted over and over in cheap paperback format for train commuters to enjoy*. And her dialogue slaps.

Austen has stayed in print because we never stopped wanting to read her tiny handful of books.

And I would just add to say, for the record, before anyone shoots me, that I do ACTUALLY ship Lizzy and Darcy like, 95% of the time.

Cough.

Tansy Rayner Roberts, November 2024

---

* See *The Lost Books of Jane Austen* by Janine Barchas (2019)

ALSO BY TANSY RAYNER ROBERTS

Time of the Cat

Castle Charming

Gorgons Deserve Nice Things

TEACUP MAGIC

Tea & Sympathetic Magic

The Frost Fair Affair

Spellcracker's Honeymoon

Lady Liesl's Seaside Surprise

Have Spirit, Will Duchess

This Enchanted Island

MUSKETEER SPACE

Musketeer Space

Joyeux

SPARKS & PHILTRES

Gate Sinister

House Perilous

Land Glorious

BELLADONNA U

Unreal Alchemy

Holiday Brew

Practical Witching

THE CREATURE COURT

Power & Majesty

The Shattered City

Reign of Beasts

Cabaret of Monsters

Siren Beat

Of Knives & Night-blooms

Love & Romanpunk

Merry Happy Valkyrie

Splashdance Silver

Liquid Gold

Ink Black Magic

NON-FICTION & ESSAYS

Pratchett's Women: Unauthorised Essays

From Baby Brain to Writer Brain: Writing Through A World
Of Parenting Distractions

It's Raining Musketeers